The
SECRET
PROJECT
NOTEBOOK

The
SECRET
PROJECT
NOTEBOOK

Carolyn Reeder

Los Alamos Historical Society
Los Alamos, New Mexico
2005

Cover art by Carol Schwartz

Library of Congress Cataloging-in-Publication Data

Reeder, Carolyn.
  The secret project notebook / Carolyn Reeder.-- 1st ed.
      p. cm.
  Summary: Moving with his parents to a remote New Mexico
location in the 1940s, twelve-year-old Fritz becomes
suspicious about his father's secret work and begins to keep
notes about events unfolding at the end of World War II.

  ISBN 0-941232-33-6

  [1. Atomic bomb--Fiction. 2. World War II, 1939-1945--
Fiction. 3. New Mexico--History--20th century--Fiction.]
I. Title.
PZ7.R235237Sec 2005
[Fic]--dc22

                         2005019166

Printed in Canada

For Liz Reeder

Author's Note

Instead of today's *Native American* and *Hispanic*, I have used *Indian* and *Spanish-American* in this story because those were the words used in the 1940s.

All of my characters are fictitious, and none of them is intended to represent any actual person. Although several well-known people are mentioned by characters in *The Secret Project Notebook*, they have no role in the story.

I have taken a few minor liberties with school life in the "secret city" during 1944–45, including omitting the late-afternoon PE classes.

Chapter One

Finally, we're almost there—wherever "there" is. I've been marking our route on state road maps for days, all the way from our neighborhood to this mesa we're driving up now, creeping along a narrow dirt road with a cliff rising on our right and nothing but the view on our left. And I mean *nothing*. Not even a guardrail.

I stick my head out the open window and crane my neck to look up, hoping for a glimpse of the mesa's flat top, but all I see is a couple of scrubby evergreens hanging onto the steep, rocky slope. I'll have to find out what kind of trees those are, 'cause they don't look like any of the ones we have back home.

"Rule 17," Dad says. "Keep all body parts inside vehicle."

"Are you sure that's not Rule 71?" I ask him.

Mom sighs. "Honestly, you two." I guess she doesn't like to be reminded of the way I used to twist numbers and letters around when I was younger. Or else she still hasn't forgiven Dad for letting Vivian move in with Grandma instead of making her come out here with us.

I think Viv's crazy, giving up an opportunity like this just so she can keep on taking violin lessons. And so she won't have to change schools. I wouldn't miss this for anything. How many twelve-year-old kids get a chance to live in a place that's so secret your parents won't even tell you where you're going till you're practically there?

And as for changing schools, that's a real plus. I can make a fresh start. I'll get to meet some new kids—some kids who don't know every single embarrassing thing I've done since kindergarten, kids who won't keep reminding me of a lot of dumb stuff I'd rather forget. Stuff from a long time ago, like how I messed up the only line I had in the third grade play.

Boy, this winding road is making me carsick. "Hey, Dad," I say, leaning forward to tap him on the shoulder. "All of a sudden I don't feel so good."

"Rule One: No throwing up in the car. Rule One supersedes all other rules including Rule 17," Dad says as he pulls over and slows to a stop. "Try to wait till some of this dust settles before you get out."

I'm standing on the side of the road—the side next to the cliff wall, not the one with the drop-off—breathing deeply—when my eyes light on this really unusual-looking rock. I pick it up and can't believe how light it is for its size. It's like pumice, except for being sort of a tan color instead of grayish.

"All right, Franklin," Mom calls. "If you feel well enough to collect rocks, you feel well enough to ride."

She's using that "or else" tone of voice, so I get back in the car, bringing the rock with me. While we're out here, I'm going to start a collection of New Mexico rocks and minerals. Hope I can find a book to help me identify them.

Pretty soon the car slows to a stop, and I see this high chain-link fence up ahead. It's got strands of barbed wire strung across the top and a couple of guards at the entrance looking like they mean business. Looking like they think we're spies sent to infiltrate this place.

One of the guards comes over to check the papers we picked up in Santa Fe, and I see that he's wearing an arm band with the letters MP. Military police! I'm puzzling over this when he glances into the back seat. He takes a second look and gets this real alert expression on his face—like now he *knows* we're spies.

"What's that you've got, kid?" His voice sounds sort of like machine-gun fire.

"You mean this rock?"

He shakes his head. "That map on the seat beside you. Hand it over." I pass it to him, and he takes one look and beckons to one of the other military policemen, an older guy. When *he* looks at the map his eyebrows go up so high they disappear under his helmet before they sag back into a frown.

"Park over there," the MP orders Dad, pointing to the right, and when Dad turns off the ignition, the older MP opens the car door and says, "Follow me." My mouth goes dry when the first guy falls into step behind the two of them, making kind of a dad sandwich.

When Dad and the MPs disappear into the guardhouse, I turn to Mom. "What the heck's going on? How come those guys are so upset about my map?"

"I have no idea, but I'm sure your father will straighten everything out," she says, but her words sound a lot braver than her voice does.

We stare in the direction of the guardhouse for so long I can't help but ask, "You don't think they're going to arrest him, do you?

"I hardly think so, hon. He hasn't done anything

3

they could arrest him for." Finally, Dad and the MPs come out of the guardhouse. They stand by the door for a minute while the older guy finishes his lecture. Then they all glance toward the car, and Dad nods his head a couple of times. When he starts toward us, I feel a little better—until I see the grim look on his face.

"What was that all about, Verne?" Mom asks him.

"It was about your son drawing that poor excuse for a road up the mesa onto the map I gave him—and then making a dot which he labeled 'Site Y.'"

Uh-oh. Whenever I'm "your son" instead of "Franklin," I'm in real trouble.

Dad tilts his rearview mirror so he can see into the back seat, and then he sort of impales me with his gaze. "Look at me, Franklin," he says as my eyes start to slide away from his. When I manage to meet Dad's eyes in the mirror, he says, "Apparently I didn't make clear to you the importance of secrecy—or the extent to which secrecy will be enforced here."

"But what did I *do*, Dad?"

"Think a minute. If you're half as smart as I think you are, you should be able to figure it out." Dad frowns, and I know he's trying to look fierce, but he has the wrong kind of face for that.

"Well, it obviously had something to do with the map."

Dad says, "It has to do with what you marked on the map."

Now I'm really puzzled. "You mean the route we followed? I don't see—"

"Not only did you draw in the road we followed up the mesa, you also wrote in 'Site Y' beside a dot you placed with surprising accuracy," Dad says, inter-

4

rupting. "You pinpointed the location of the laboratory even though I told you that everything about it was top secret."

"But—"

"There are no 'buts,' Franklin. Once we go through that gate you'll be on a military base, and you'll have to obey the rules without questioning them, whether you like them or not, and whether you think they're fair or not. Do you understand?"

His tone of voice tells me I'd better understand. "Yeah, I guess so, but how can I obey the rules if nobody tells me what they are?"

Mom says, "That's a fair question, Verne."

"All right, then. For starters, people up here just call this place 'the Hill,' and we all use the address Post Office Box 1663, Santa Fe." I start to say something, but Dad's not finished. "If we go to Santa Fe, we aren't to talk to anyone there—other than making a purchase or transacting business, of course—and there will be security personnel checking to make sure we don't."

"Boy, this is going to be like living in a spy thriller!"

Instead of answering, Dad readjusts his rearview mirror and starts the car again. As we pull through the gate, I can feel those MPs following us with their eyes, which makes me feel half excited and half scared. Or maybe 90 percent excited and 10 percent scared.

Pretty soon we stop again—to get our passes, Dad tells us, and I don't think anything about that till they *fingerprint* us.

Then this WAC says, "Come with me, please," and the next thing I know she's handing me a comb and

5

pointing to a mirror. "Make yourself presentable so I can take your picture."

I don't have to look in the mirror to know she's talking about the way my hair sort of stands up instead of lying flat. "Sorry, ma'am, but this is as presentable as I get." Too bad I didn't inherit Dad's naturally wavy hair, or even Mom's silky-smooth hair that does whatever she wants it to. Mine's dark brown like theirs, but that's where the similarity ends.

The WAC shrugs and motions me to a chair. I'm still blinking from the flash bulb when she asks if I've got any scars or other identifying marks on my body.

"Only this little scar on my arm." I show her, and she makes a note of it. "What do you need to know that for?" I ask.

"For identification purposes," she says. "You may go now."

We're back in the car before it sinks in that they'd only need to identify me by scars and other marks on my body if I was dead. What kind of place has Dad brought us to, anyway? I lean forward and tap his shoulder. "What the heck are we doing on a military base? You said we were moving here so you could work in a science lab."

"It's a government laboratory, Franklin," Dad says as he starts the car, "and it's located on a military base for security reasons. I think I've already explained that our work must be done in complete secrecy." From the way he said that, I can tell Dad's still mad at me, and I'm kind of surprised, 'cause he's usually pretty easygoing.

We all crank our windows shut to keep out the dust stirred up by a line of dump trucks coming toward us, and I wonder how Dad can see to drive. I'm thinking this place looks like one huge construction site when we pass rows and rows of trailers, all painted army green. "Hey, are we going to live in one of those?"

"Over my dead body," Mom says.

Dad says, "The trailers are for the construction and maintenance workers. Scientists' families are assigned to apartments a little farther on."

"Away from all this dust, I hope," Mom says.

"I think you'll like the apartment, Mona. The living room has a fireplace and a fine view of the mountains. We'll share a balcony with the other family that lives upstairs."

I'm wondering if Mom noticed he didn't say it was away from the dust when I see a bunch of green, two-story buildings with balconies ahead of us. Sure enough, pretty soon Dad pulls up alongside one of them and says, "Well, troops, we're home."

Mom's looking at the packed dirt where a lawn ought to be, so I guess she's figured out that the apartments aren't away from all the dust. Dad and I climb out of the car, but Mom doesn't open her door until a woman and her little kid come out of a downstairs apartment and hurry toward us.

The woman says, "Hi! You must be the Maddens. I'm Sally Edwards, and this is Timmy. I've got a pot of coffee and a pitcher of lemonade ready to pour, and Pamela next door baked a batch of cookies this morning. You all come on down as soon as you've looked over your new place—upstairs on the left."

Without waiting to hear anything more, I dash up the outside stairway and along the balcony to our apartment. It's unlocked, and the first thing I see when I go inside is the vase of wildflowers somebody's put on the coffee table.

I go into the kitchen, and after I check to make sure the calendar on the wall is turned to September 1944, I notice a loaf of bread, a plate of cookies, and a jar of grape jelly on the counter with a note that says, "Welcome to the Hill!" Out of habit, I open the fridge, and there's a quart bottle of milk, a platter of fried chicken, and a huge bowl of potato salad in there.

I'm making myself welcome with a couple of cookies when I hear my parents come in. "Guess what?" I say, going to meet them. "Somebody left our supper in the fridge."

Mom's got this kind of dazed look on her face as she glances around, taking in the army-issue furniture and then this monstrous black *wood* stove—or maybe coal stove—in the middle of the kitchen. Dad looks nervous, and I realize he's waiting for Mom to say something about this place he's brought us to, the place where we'll be living until the war's over.

Actually, we're both waiting for Mom to say something. I guess she must be practicing what she preaches: If you can't say something nice, don't say anything at all. I've heard her tell my sister that about a thousand times.

Dad and I follow Mom down the hall and into each of the two small bedrooms, and then we all look through the door of the tiny bathroom. No tub—only an ugly concrete shower. I wait for Mom to say something about that, but she just frowns. She's actually kind of pretty, in a comfortable sort of way, but you'd never guess it when she's frowning.

We follow her back to the living room, and when her eyes come to rest on that bouquet somebody picked, she takes a deep breath and says, "At least we have good neighbors."

Chapter Two

Boy, there's nothing like getting here one day and starting school the next. It's a good thing the trip didn't take us any longer.

This is a great school—brand new last year—and every room has a whole wall of windows with a view of the mountains. The classes are a lot smaller here than back home, so you don't get that crowded feeling.

So far I like all my teachers, especially this one. Mrs. Jackson, her name is. With that mop of dark curls she looks more like somebody's big sister than a teacher, but she's been pretty efficient at getting all the first-day-of-school business taken care of so we can get to work.

Mrs. Jackson flips her map chart to the Southwest. "Okay, class," she says, "in social studies this year we're going to start by learning about New Mexico—its history, its geography, and its culture."

The words pop out before I can stop them. "New Mexico's got *culture*?"

The kids laugh, but Mrs. Jackson ignores them. "It certainly does, Franklin," she says. "This area's culture predates the settlements at Jamestown and Massachusetts Bay by centuries." Everybody stops laughing to stare at her, and she explains, "You probably think that 'culture' means the fine arts. Things like concerts and plays and art exhibits."

"Or something biologists grow in a petri dish," I say, and the kid behind me groans. Uh-oh. I'm supposed to be making a fresh start.

Mrs. Jackson ignores the groaning, too. "That's one meaning of the word, Franklin," she says, "but we're going to be studying the culture of the early people of New Mexico—their arts, their religion, their agricultural practices, and their government."

"You mean the Indians?" I ask her. I never knew they had government.

Behind me, somebody mutters, "This kid sure does like to hear himself talk," but Mrs. Jackson doesn't seem to notice.

"The Indians, and the Spanish-Americans, too," she says.

I notice that the bored-looking, dark-haired boy slouched in a seat at the end of the front row shows a hint of interest. Apparently Mrs. Jackson notices, too, because she zeroes in on him and says, "Manny, can you tell us when the Spanish first came to this area?"

"Back in the 1500s," he says. "They set up missions to convert the Indians to Christianity."

The teacher thanks Manny like he'd done something special and then asks the class, "Who would like to come up to the map and show us where this mesa of ours is located?" I sort of clench my jaw so I don't holler out that it's not on the map, and Mrs. Jackson calls on the only person who raised a hand— an energetic-looking girl with bobbed brown hair and bangs. Kathy.

Kathy goes up front, and I see that she's about my height, which is a little on the short side for a seventh-grade boy but seems just right for her. She

11

says, "Well, we're northwest of Santa Fe and north of Albuquerque, so we'd be right about—here."

"Good work, Kathy," Mrs. Jackson says. "And now can you tell us why a town as large as this one isn't on the map?"

"Because they want to keep the Lab a secret. Because no one is supposed to know this place even exists."

Mrs. Jackson nods, but Manny says, "Shoot, when that map was printed, there wasn't no laboratory up here. No town, neither. This time two years ago, there wasn't nothin' here but a boarding school for rich men's sons."

"You've made a good point, Manny," Mrs. Jackson says. "But even if the map had been printed yesterday, we wouldn't be on it."

I think about telling them what can happen if all you do is pencil this place onto your own personal map, but I manage to keep my mouth shut about that. I actually manage to keep it shut till the end of class, when everybody starts home for lunch.

I'm on my way out the door, thinking about the leftover fried chicken Mom said we'd finish at lunchtime, when somebody punches me on the arm and says, "What's the matter, Fritz? You deaf or something?" It's this lanky, tough-looking kid with greasy-looking blond hair.

"How was I supposed to know you meant me? My name's Franklin." And then I add, "You can call me Frank, if you want."

"Nah. I'm gonna call you Fritz," the boy says, and he turns to the scrawny kid that's with him and asks, "Hey, Red—don't you think he looks like Fritz in that comic about them Katzenjammer Kids? You know the one I mean?"

Red squints at me and says, "Yeah, I've seen it, and he does look sort of like Fritz. It's the way that dark hair of his stands up on the top of his head, right, Lonny?"

I turn away without waiting to hear Lonny's answer, but as I leave the building, he yells, "See you after lunch, Fritz." I start across the school yard, and when I hear running footsteps behind me, I steel myself for another punch.

Fortunately, it's Kathy. "Those two stirred up trouble at school all last year," she says when she catches up. "Just ignore them."

"You sound like my mom. I'd rather take my dad's advice—it worked pretty well back at my old school." Kathy looks interested, so I tell her. "Dad says when somebody teases you, you've got to figure out a way to show it doesn't bother you. If you let them think they can get your goat, they'll never give you a minute's peace, so you have to sort of turn things around and take the wind out of their sails."

Kathy frowns. "I don't get it."

"Here's a for instance. Lonny and his red-haired friend called me 'Fritz,' right? Well, if I started telling everybody to call me Fritz instead of Franklin, it wouldn't be much fun for those two any more, and I wouldn't feel like I was their victim, either." Besides, kids might think twice before they tried anything with somebody named Fritz. Who sounds tougher, Fritz or Franklin?

Kathy's eyes grow wide, and she says, "But you wouldn't really change your name, would you?"

"Might as well. If those two keep calling me Fritz,

13

the other kids are going to pick it up anyway. That's the way it always works." After a few more steps, I add, "I should have kept my big mouth shut in class."

"You have to participate if you want to get A's," Kathy says. "Besides, those guys have a grudge against us anyway." I'm wondering who she means by *us* when she adds, "They don't like it that scientists' families live in apartments and they're stuck in trailers or Quonset huts. Places without bathrooms."

I can feel my eyebrows shoot up. "No bathrooms? You've got to be kidding!"

Kathy shakes her head. "Nope. They've got bath houses that everybody shares."

I'm really glad we're almost to my building, because I'm not used to discussing bathrooms with girls. "Well, this is where I live. See you later."

I head for the kitchen, where Mom's spooning potato salad onto our plates next to the fried chicken I'd been thinking about. "Hi, Franklin. How was your morning?"

I pull out a chair and say, "It was fine. From now on, though, I want you to call me Fritz."

Mom frowns. "If you want a nickname, what's wrong with 'Frank'? I think you'll be letting yourself in for a rough time if you choose something that sounds as German as 'Fritz.' I can't imagine why—"

"Mom. You know how my hair sort of stands up because of that cowlick I've got? Sort of like Fritz in that comic strip? The Katzenjammer Kids?"

A look of understanding crosses her face. "So you're fighting fire with fire, like your dad's taught you to. I hope—"

"Looks like a good lunch, Mom," I say as she

14

pours my milk.

Apparently she realizes I don't want to hear what she hopes, because she drops that subject and says, "After today you might have to fix your own lunch sometimes, Franklin."

"Fritz," I remind her. "How come?"

"Because I've got a job over at the Tech Area."

"No kidding! A job doing what, Mom?"

"I'll be secretary for—well, for one of the scientists."

I put down my milk glass and ask, "Don't you know which one yet?"

"I know which one, Franklin."

"Fritz," I say automatically. "Are you trying to tell me that you can't even let your own son know who your boss is?"

Instead of answering, she says, "I'll probably take a sandwich to eat at my desk most days, at least until I've dealt with all the work that's been piling up."

I'm beginning to see what Dad meant about secrecy. "Well, I'd better start back so I'm not late for my afternoon classes." And so I don't have to walk back with Kathy. The last thing I need is for those guys to start teasing me about my "girlfriend."

I'm starting home at the end of the school day when Kathy catches up to me and says, "Hey, are you any good at ping-pong?"

I allow as how I'm not too bad at it, and she says, "Want to try a game or two over at the PX?"

"What's the PX?" I ask. She gives me this shocked look, so I remind her that I only got here yesterday afternoon.

"P for Post, X for Exchange," Kathy explains. "It's

kind of a combination store, snack bar, and place for off-duty soldiers to relax and have a good time, but anybody can go there. This early, the ping-pong table's probably free. Come on."

I don't remember actually saying I was going to play, but there's nothing else to do—and nobody else to do it with—so, what the heck.

We go inside the PX, and my mouth falls open when I see all the candy bars and packs of chewing gum lined up along the counter near the cashier. "Hershey bars! I don't think I've seen one of those since the first year of the war." I fish in my pocket and find a nickel, and as soon as I've paid I start tearing off the wrapper. "Want some?" I ask, hoping she's allergic to chocolate.

"Maybe a couple of squares," she says, so I break two of them off for her and then fold the next four into a cube and pop it in my mouth. Kathy grins and says, "You look like you just died and went to heaven. They've got a lot of stuff here and at the commissary—that's the grocery store the army runs—that you can't buy other places 'cause of wartime shortages. My Dad says the army tries to keep the people here satisfied by 'catering to their creature comforts.' Come on, before somebody else gets that ping-pong table."

We hit the ball back and forth for a while, and when that starts to get tiresome, I say, "Want to try a game? You can serve first."

Kathy catches the ball I toss her. "Ready?" she asks.

I nod, and—Holy cow! That ball whizzed past before I had a chance to raise my paddle! One of the GIs over by the pinball machines tosses the ball back to me, and I toss it to Kathy. Her second serve is exactly like the first, but this time I manage to get a swing at it.

I connect with the third serve, but the ball fwops into the net. This is pitiful—I'm being smeared! I manage to return her next serve, but she's put so much spin on it that I miss her side of the table completely. Gotta get this last one. I'm sort of crouched down, waiting for it to come zinging at me, and she does this totally different kind of serve that drops the ball up close to the net.

"Zero serving five," Kathy says. She's got this deadpan look on her face, but it's pretty obvious she's enjoying herself. Well, I've got a fierce serve, so now's my chance to catch up. I give the ball a top spin, but she slams it back, and she's got this triumphant tone in her voice when she calls the score. "Zero, six."

I take a deep breath and look at the left side of the table, then serve a fast one to the right side. She hits it, and as the ball arcs over the net, I see my chance for a slam. But instead of a normal bounce, the ball hits the table and makes a bunch of little hops.

"Zero, seven. Game's over," Kathy says, setting down her paddle.

"Over! But—"

"It's a skunk game, Fritz. If the score is 7-0 or 11-1, the losing player's 'skunked' and you don't bother to play to 21. Come on, let's go."

We cut across a nearly empty dance floor and pass a table where older kids are drinking cokes. "I thought you told me you were good at ping-pong," Kathy says as we go outside.

First she beats me, and then she rubs it in. "I said I was good at ping-pong, not excellent at it. Who taught you to play like that, anyway?"

"My brother. Matthew hasn't lost a ping-pong game since he was fifteen. Not that he's had a chance to play lately—he's overseas."

"Atlantic theater or Pacific?"

Kathy says shortly, "He's fighting in Italy."

"Atlantic theater, then," I say.

"I hate all this talk about 'theaters,' like Matthew's over there watching a play instead of risking his life."

Since her voice is kind of shaky, I go back to the subject of ping-pong. "How come you just pitty-patted around when we were volleying, Kathy?"

"Why do you think? 'Cause I didn't want to give you a chance to figure out how to return my shots."

Not much chance of that. Oh, well. At least nobody from school saw me being smeared.

When I get home, Mom's sitting on the balcony with a pad of paper on her lap. Writing to Grandma and Vivian, I'll bet. "Looks like you've found a friend," she says.

"Not exactly, Mom."

"At least you have somebody to walk to and from school with. How did your first day go, hon?"

"About like you'd expect."

Mom frowns, like she's trying to decide exactly how I meant that, so I figure I'd better distract her. "Remember that rock I picked up when Dad stopped the car yesterday?" I ask. "It's 'volcanic tuff.' I found a book in the school library that's got a whole section on—get this—The Recent Volcanic History of New Mexico." I guess their idea of recent is a lot different from mine.

"You like the school, then?"

18

So much for distracting her. "School's fine, Mom." Actually, school *is* fine. There's always going to be a couple of kids you wish went to some other school—reform school, maybe. I'm just glad Lonny and Red are only in one of my classes.

Chapter Three

It feels sort of strange to start out for school without Mom telling me to have a good day—but no stranger than it felt when she went off to her first day at work this morning looking as excited as I felt on the first day of school. Boy, that seems a lot longer ago than yesterday.

I'm halfway down the steps when I see Kathy coming, and she's already seen me, so I can't duck back inside till she's gone past.

"Hi, Fritz," Kathy calls, and I decide that since Lonny and his pal are going to tease me anyhow, I might as well walk with her. I'm kind of pleased that she used my new name without being reminded.

"What did you write your homework composition on?" I ask her as we set off. "I did mine on the places I want to go while we're out here—the Petrified Forest and the Grand Canyon in Arizona, and then down to Mexico. I figure if we save up our gasoline ration stamps, we could manage all that."

Kathy's shaking her head, so I argue, "I know we're not supposed to travel because of the war, but it's not like we'd be going by bus or train and taking up space a soldier on leave could use to get home."

"You might as well forget it, Fritz," Kathy says. "In the first place, scientists at the Lab don't take vacations—they all work six days a week, including holidays like Labor Day and New Year's. And in the second place, we aren't allowed to go any farther than a hundred miles from here. It's one of the rules."

I stare at her, wondering if Dad knew about all this when he agreed to come here. I'll bet Mom didn't.

"I wrote a fake 'What I Did on My Vacation' composition," Kathy says. "I put in all this stuff about going to the shore and visiting my grandparents, and I ended it with 'and then I woke up here on the Hill.'"

I don't answer, 'cause we're almost to the school yard, and Lonny and Red are hanging around, looking this way.

"Hey, Fritz!" Lonny hollers. "Who's your girlfriend?"

"This is Kathy," I holler back. "Who's *your* girlfriend?"

That stops him for a minute, but then he says, "Red and I don't have girlfriends."

"Hey, that's too bad," I say as Kathy and I walk up to them. Lonny and Red look at each other and then look back at us. They can't seem to think of anything to say, which is fine with me.

The bell sounds, and the two of them dash to the building. As Kathy and I walk toward the door, she says, "If they're going to carry on like that, maybe you'd rather not walk to school with me."

She should have thought about that sooner. "Don't worry about it," I tell her as we go inside. "Those two are going to have it in for me no matter who I walk with."

My morning classes seem to crawl by, but it's finally time for social studies—the one class I have with Lonny and Red. Mrs. Jackson starts to call the roll, and each person answers "present" until she calls

"Franklin?"

Before I can say what I'd planned to, Red calls out, "You mean 'Fritz,' don't you?"

A couple of people snicker, but they shut up fast when I say, "He's right, Mrs. Jackson. I've decided to go by my nickname this year. I want everybody to call me Fritz."

Mrs. Jackson looks from me to Red, and then back to me again. She seems sort of uncertain, so I say, "I'd like you to change my name to 'Fritz' in your roll book, ma'am. All my other teachers have." I asked each of them privately, before class started, but I wanted to make things really clear to Lonny and Red—and Red played right into my hands.

There's complete silence in the room while Mrs. Jackson makes the change in her attendance book, and it takes all my self-control not to turn around to see how Lonny and Red are reacting. I figure Kathy will tell me.

When class is over, Mrs. Jackson asks me to stay behind. "Are you sure you want to be called Fritz?" she asks.

I meet her worried eyes and say, "Yes, ma'am. I'm sure."

She looks at me for a moment—her eyes are a deep blue color, with long dark lashes—before she says, "All right, then. You may go."

Kathy's waiting at the door, and she says, "You should have seen their faces! They couldn't believe what they were hearing."

"Now what do you think of my dad's advice?" I ask her.

"It sure worked today," Kathy says, and I kind of

like the way she's looking at me now. With respect. Maybe I still have a chance to make a fresh start.

After school, I decide to explore the meadow Mom said she walked to yesterday afternoon—when the walls of the apartment started to close in on her, as she put it. I figure a meadow ought to have some interesting plants for me to identify and add to Notes on Flora and Fauna—the notebook I started when we visited Grandma Madden in Michigan last summer.

I find the notebook and the copies of *Guide to Southwestern Plants* and *Birds of New Mexico* that I borrowed from the school library, grab an apple and a couple of fig bars, and I'm on my way.

I'm trying to identify the small yellow blossoms growing along the bridle path that goes through the meadow when I hear hoofbeats. I look up and see Manny, the Spanish-American kid who's in almost all my classes, coming toward me on this huge black horse.

"Holy cow!" I say when they stop. "How many hands high is he, anyway?" Thanks to my sister's constant talk about horses, I know enough not to ask how tall he is.

"Almost seventeen hands. Nice, ain't he? I call him Coal Dust."

"Is he yours?"

Manny shakes his head. "I don't own him, but I ride him all the time. Anybody can ride them army horses they've got back there in the stable. And now I got a question for you, Fritz. What the heck are you doin' out here with a book?"

"Trying to identify some of the plants that don't

grow where I'm from."

"You don't need no book," Manny says scornfully. "Just ask me."

I look up at him, not sure whether he's serious, and he gestures at the patch of orange flowers a little way off the path and says, "That there's Indian paintbrush." And then he tells me the name of the yellow blooms I was trying to identify when he rode up.

I open my Flora and Fauna notebook, and Manny watches me write down what he told me. When I finish, he says, "You're different from most of them Anglos, you know?"

"Different how?"

Manny shrugs. "You don't come here acting like anything you don't already know ain't worth knowing. And you got respect for living things." His face clouds over, and he says, "You shoulda seen this mesa before they started ripping it up with machines and putting all them ugly green buildings everywhere."

"How long have you lived around here, anyhow?"

"My whole life. And five or six generations of my family before me. Until the army came along and bought up our land so they could ruin it."

Before I can think of something to say to that, Manny digs his heels into the horse's flanks and rides off. It's getting late, so I start on back, reminding myself that Dad asked me to stop by the PX and get him a newspaper.

I'm in line, watching all the activity while I wait my turn to pay—soldiers and WACs jitterbugging or playing ping-pong, the crowded snack bar, some housewife buying stamps—when I spot Lonny and Red. They're playing one of the pinball machines, and

I'm feeling grateful that (1) they're on the other side of the small dance floor and (2) they haven't seen me.

But then Lonny looks up. I watch him say something to Red and then start to saunter over in my direction. I've got my money ready, but the WAC in front of me is flirting with the cashier. When she finally leaves, I plunk down my coins and head for the door. Soon as I'm outside, I take off for home—not running, exactly. Just walking fast, like I'm in a big hurry.

I'm almost home when I catch up to Dad. "Hi, kiddo," he says. "I was thinking about you. How'd you like to explore some of the Indian ruins around here?"

"That would be great, Dad. When?"

"With a six-day work week, we're pretty much limited to Sundays, aren't we?"

That's not the kind of question that needs an answer, so I say, "I'll have to start a new notebook on ancient Indians—guess I'd better buy one of those composition books they sell at the PX."

Dad gets a dollar from his billfold and hands it to me. "Might as well stock up on them," he says. "You're bound to find a lot of things that interest you out here."

"Thanks, Dad," I say, glad that he didn't make me ask him for money or else spend my allowance. After I get the notebooks, I'll stock up on chocolate bars, too.

Chapter Four

I'm looking out the living room window, admiring the dusting of snow on the tops of those mountains to the west, when Mom comes to the kitchen door and says, "That view almost makes up for the town being such a drab, ugly place, doesn't it?" She raises her voice and calls, "Breakfast, Verne."

I'm already at the table when Dad comes into the kitchen. "Well, Franklin," he says, "you're looking wide-awake this morning."

"Remember, Dad—I'm Fritz now."

He frowns. "I'm not sure you should allow those young toughs to rename you like this."

"But that's the whole point, Dad—I'm renaming myself. You know, taking the wind out of their sails."

"My own words, coming back to haunt me," Dad says, and then he gives an exaggerated sigh.

Mom pours herself another cup of coffee. "Go ahead and be Fritz at school, if you must, but be Franklin here at home, hon."

"A good compromise, Mona," Dad says as he passes her the milk.

It's not a compromise at all. They get their way, I don't get my way. "I disagree, Verne," I tell him. Dad's spoon stops halfway to his mouth, and I say, "See how you feel when somebody calls you by a different name than you want them to? Even though your name

26

really is Verne, that's not what you want me to call you, so—"

"You've made your point, *Fritz*," Dad says.

I'm feeling pretty good until Mom says, "I don't believe this, Verne. I don't believe you're actually—"

"Mona. Which would you have me do, focus my energy on my work at the Lab, or waste it bickering with a twelve-year-old?"

Mom sighs. "You're right, of course. In the great scheme of things, this isn't worth arguing about." She carries her dishes to the sink and turns the water on full force. I'm about to remind her that we're supposed to be conserving water, but I decide not to.

"You know what's strange?" I ask Kathy as we walk home at lunchtime. "I feel sort of like I've always lived here. Like I've always gone to this school. Like I've always been called Fritz."

Kathy nods. "I know what you mean. This place is so different from what we're used to, it seems like a whole new life. And you know what else? If you do anything once here, it becomes a tradition."

"You mean like the two of us walking to and from school together?" I ask, half teasing, half serious.

"Look, Fritz, if you don't want to walk with me—"

"Don't be silly, Kath. It's a tradition, remember?" Actually, it's not all that bad. "I'll wait for you after lunch," I say, just to make sure she knows I was joking. Mostly, anyhow.

The minute I open the door to our apartment, I know somebody's been here. There's this smell, kind of a clean smell. Floor wax, that's what it is. I head for the kitchen and stop short in the doorway when I

27

see this Indian woman eating her lunch at our table.

She smiles and points to herself. "I'm Juanita," she says.

So I point to myself and say, "I'm Fritz." I can hardly believe there's a real live Indian, sitting right here in our kitchen! I'm making mental notes—hair pulled back, bangs, a colorful scarf thing hanging over her shoulder—when I realize I'm staring. So I go to the cupboard for a plate and a glass, pour some milk, grab a loaf of bread from the bread box, find the peanut butter and jelly, and make a couple trips to the table.

I get a knife and start to make a sandwich, and now Juanita's the one who's staring. Or maybe just watching intently. After I cut the sandwich in half I have an idea. "Want to trade?"

She frowns and repeats, "Trade?"

I pass her the plate and say, "You take," and her eyes light up with understanding. She takes half the sandwich and offers me a piece of some kind of round, flat bread. I take it and say, "We trade."

While we eat, I'm thinking about all the questions I'm going to ask her, but as soon as she finishes the sandwich, she says, "I must go now."

The minute she leaves, I dash to my room and bring back one of my new composition books so I can start a notebook on Modern American Indians. I'm sitting there among the crumbs, writing down everything I remember about the way Juanita was dressed, when Mom comes in.

"Smells clean," she says. "Looks clean, too."

"There was this Indian woman named Juanita, and—"

"I meant to tell you she was coming. Army buses bring workers up here from the pueblos," Mom explains as she starts to fix her lunch. "New mothers and wives with jobs are at the top of the list for maids. Don't make yourself late getting back to school—your friend said to tell you she couldn't wait any longer, by the way."

I glance at the clock. "Yikes! See you later."

The last of the upper school kids are straggling into the building when I get there, and when I slip into my seat in math class, the teacher is about to start passing back the pop quiz she gave yesterday. She hands Manny his paper first, and after he takes a quick look, he crushes it into a wad and hurls it at the trash can. It falls short, landing in the aisle beside me. Automatically, I lean down to pick it up, then stuff the wad into the empty inkwell in the corner of my desk.

It looks like Mrs. James is one of those teachers who returns test papers in the order of their scores, starting with the lowest grade and ending with the highest. While she continues to hand back the quizzes, everybody's glancing around to see who has theirs back and who doesn't. I don't have mine yet, and she's only got two left. I'm practically holding my breath, waiting and hoping, until she gives the next-to-the-last paper to Kathy. "Congratulations, Fritz," Mrs. James says as she hands me mine.

My face feels warm, so I know I'm turning red, but for once it's not from embarrassment. I glance over at Kathy, but she's scowling down at her paper. I lean forward enough to see the big red 95% at the top—just one point less than my score—and wonder what the trouble is. Then I remember the ping-pong game. Kathy likes to win, and I guess in math, winning means having the top score.

At the end of class, Manny stops at my desk and says, "You got something of mine, Fritz." I give him a blank look, and he adds, "That paper you picked up."

His quiz paper. I point to the inkwell, and he fishes it out and crushes it into a tighter ball. "I *told* them I don't belong in no pre-algebra class, but would they listen to me?" He pitches his voice high and says, "'We're putting you in the academic classes, Manny, because you have po-TEN-tial.'"

I grin and say, "I could give you some help with the math if you want." He was friendly enough the day he was riding Coal Dust in the meadow, so why not?

"I don't take no favors. But thanks, anyhow."

"What if we sort of traded favors?" I ask, starting to get an idea.

Manny snorts. "What kind of favor could somebody like me do for somebody like you?"

"Well, my dad said something about Indian ruins around here. Since you've always lived on the mesa, maybe you could show me some of them."

Manny gives me a long look, like he's making sure I mean it, and finally, he says, "Okay. It's a deal."

"Meet me in the library after school, and we'll start out by doing our homework together." I dash to my next class, pleased with the way things are going. I'll be able to avoid Lonny and Red after school, and I'll have my own private guide to the ancient Indian sites. Not bad!

Chapter Five

Gravel from the unpaved road rattles against the underneath of the car on the drive back from this week's outing—a picnic and hike. According to Dad, different groups of scientists plan some kind of outdoor activity every Sunday. Their families come along, but it seems like the men mostly talk to each other about whatever it is they're working on in the Tech Area.

With all the fuss about secrecy, I'm kind of surprised Dad and the other guys are talking about the project when I'm in the car with them, even if they do think I'm asleep. Haven't they ever heard of playing possum?

Not that I've heard anything that makes sense. They seem to be using some kind of code—talking about "the Gadget" and "Little Boy" and "Fat Man." At first I thought they might be ribbing this big guy who's taking more than his share of the back seat, but that's probably not the sort of thing adults would do.

The car stops at the gate, and I make a show of blinking and rubbing my eyes when Dad gives me a little shake and tells me to hand up my pass to the driver. For the next couple of minutes the men don't talk about anything except where to go on next Sunday's outing. Boy, if they asked me, I'd say let's go back to the place we went today and see if we can find some more ancient Indian cliff dwellings. They were neat!

The guy driving the car pool lets Dad and me out in front of our apartment, and Mom gets out of the car behind ours, along with Timmy and his mother. We all walk to the building together, and when I start up the stairs to our apartment, Timmy calls, "Bye, Fritz."

"You seem to have made quite a hit with that little boy," Mom says.

"Yeah, he must have asked me about a hundred questions today." Still, I'd sure rather put up with Timmy's questions than with Lonny's and Red's teasing.

Dad says, "So what did you think of this week's outing, Fritz?"

"It was great! I added two more kinds of trees to my Flora and Fauna notebook, and I made a diagram of those pueblo ruins at the bottom of the canyon, too. Want to see it?" We stop on the balcony so I can show him, and then he looks at the list of plants I've identified since we've been here.

As soon as I'm inside, I make a beeline for my room and the stack of composition notebooks I bought at the PX. I take two of them to my desk, set one aside and write NOTES ON ANCIENT INDIANS on the cover of the other. Then I copy the rough diagram of the pueblo onto the first page and label it "Pueblo ruins found in Bandelier National Monument, N.M., Fall of 1944." On the next page I write down everything the ranger I talked to told me about the people who used to live there.

When I'm finished, I put that notebook aside and pick up the other one. I hold it for a moment, trying to decide what to call it. Facts about the Secret Project? Fat chance I'd get any facts. Maybe *Notes* would be better. I'm about to letter that on the front of the notebook when something tells me not to. Instead, I open it to the first page and print NOTES ON THE SECRET PROJECT in the center.

On the page after that I write CODES on the top line and list the three pairs of words the scientists kept using: the Gadget, Little Boy, and Fat Man. So what else do I know? Not much. Only the names of a few scientists, but every little bit helps. I head the next page PERSONNEL and start listing all the scientists I know, starting with Dad. It's not a very long list, but it's a start.

It looks pretty dumb, though, just a list of names, but what else do I know about them? Heck, what do I know about my own dad? Only that he's a physicist and has a white badge, which means he's cleared for all the secret stuff, not just the secret stuff he's working on, like the guys with blue badges are.

I bend over the page and write in three headings across the first line: NAME, SCIENCE, and BADGE COLOR, and then I fill in the odds and ends of things I know. Not many entries, lots of blank spaces, but it's a start. Too bad the men don't wear their badges on the outings.

Actually, it would be kind of fun to see how much I can find out by keeping my eyes and ears open, like I did today. By golly, I'm going to do it!

"Gotta go to school now, Timmy," I say, tossing him his ball, and as he runs after it I get my books from the bottom step. I manage to say "Hi" to Kathy and listen for a couple of minutes while she tells me what her brother wrote about in his latest letter before I ask, "By the way, what color badge does your dad have?"

"A white one. Why?"

"Um, 'cause I bet somebody your dad was a chemist with a white badge. Yeah, that's why."

Kathy says, "You know, Fritz, you're a terrible liar."

I can feel my face getting red. "Actually, it's sort of a secret."

"I can keep a secret as well as you can, Fritz."

Probably better, 'cause I can feel this one getting ready to slip out. "You promise?" I ask, and when she nods, I tell her. "I'm working on this chart, see—it's a list of the scientists who work here, their badge colors, and what each one's branch of science is."

Kathy gives me a funny look. "Did somebody ask you to do that?"

"Somebody like a German spy? I'm not stupid, you know. See, I've got this notebook, and I'm calling it Notes on the Secret Project. Just for fun, I'm writing down anything I can find out about what's going on here, and one of my categories is Personnel."

"My father's not a chemist, he's in ordnance." Kathy says.

"I thought that was laws and stuff. Like the ordinance about dogs not running loose."

Kathy gives me a disgusted look and says, "You're thinking of *or–din–ance*. Three syllables. *Ord–nance* has to do with explosives."

All of a sudden I start to understand why we aren't supposed to talk to anybody if we go to Santa Fe. We could give secrets away without even knowing it—like the fact that the scientists up here are working on something to do with explosives. Wait till I put *that* in my new notebook.

"Listen, Fritz, I can give you the names and badge colors of the other scientists in our building if you want."

"Hey, that would be swell! We can—" I break off when I see Lonny and Red lurking around the edge of the playground.

Red hollers, "Here comes Fritz with his girlfriend," but nobody pays any attention.

"Haven't you two got yourselves girlfriends yet?" I ask him.

"We don't want no girlfriends," Lonny says.

I give him an amused look and say, "That's just sour grapes."

"What's that supposed to mean?"

"You mean you've never heard the fable of the fox and the grapes?" I can't keep the astonishment out of my voice, and boy, does that ever rub Lonny the wrong way. He looks like he's going to slug me, but at the sound of the bell he charges off toward the door instead.

Kathy watches Lonny and Red push their way through the crowd of boys funneling into the building. "How come they're always in such a hurry to go inside?" she asks.

I shrug. "They probably figure they can't be the best, but they might have a chance at being first."

"Then I guess the reason you don't do it is because you think you're the best," Kathy says.

Her snotty tone of voice gets my goat, and I hear myself say, "Getting the highest grade on the math quiz doesn't necessarily mean I'm the best, Kath."

She scowls and says, "Just remember, Fritz, I'm a lot closer to being the best at math than you are to being the best at ping-pong."

Talk about hitting below the belt! "You know, Kathy," I say as we go into the building, "there's something important your brother forgot to teach you."

"What?" she asks, sounding indignant.

I look her right in the eye and say, "That real winners don't brag." She gets this shocked expression on her face, and before she can say anything, I start down the hall to class. For a couple of seconds I feel pretty good, but then I start to wish I'd kept my big mouth shut. It was dumb to let her get to me with that crack about ping-pong, and even dumber to bring up the math quiz in the first place. Oh, well. I've never claimed to be a winner, real or otherwise.

I finish helping Manny with his math homework in the library after school, and as we're leaving the building we see two kids shooting baskets. They call out something in Spanish, and Manny answers, then turns to me and says, "You don't play ball, do you?"

" 'Course I do." Dad made sure of that.

Manny looks like he doesn't believe me, but he says, "Come on, then."

One of the kids is really good, but I'm no worse than Manny and the other guy. We play around for a while, and when I look at my watch, I say, "Holy cow! Look at the time—I'm supposed to be somewhere."

I head for the Tech Area, figuring it's late enough that Mom's already started home, but I'll still be able to watch a lot of the scientists leave and notice the badge color of anybody I recognize. I lean against a car that's parked near the gate and try to look bored, like maybe I'm waiting for somebody.

First, a lot of younger guys and some WACs come pouring out, with some other women sprinkled in—scientists' wives who work there, I guess. All of them have orange badges like Mom's. I wait a while longer, and a couple of guys with blue badges come out. *Bingo!* I met one of them on Sunday's hike. He's George Somebody-or-other, and he's got on a blue badge.

"Hey, Fritz," he says, coming over to where I'm lounging. "What's new?"

"Nothing much. I'm just waiting for my dad."

George says, "You might have a long wait. He looked pretty involved when I last saw him." He turns to his companion. "Sam, this is Verne Madden's son." We say the usual polite things while I make a mental note: George and Sam, blue badges.

After they leave, I don't see anybody else I recognize, so I head for the PX to buy Dad's newspaper, kind of pleased that I got another name and two badge colors for my list and wondering how to find out what kind of scientists they are. I'm almost to the door when somebody yells, "Hey, Fritzy-Witzy!"

Lonny and Red. I pretend I didn't hear, but once I'm inside, I duck into the men's room to get away from them. The place is empty, and I realize too late that if those two come in here looking for me, they'll have me cornered.

Suddenly I know what to do. One of the stalls has an "Out of Order" sign taped to its door, so I lock myself inside, sit on the toilet seat, and press my feet against the door to make sure they don't show underneath. Just in time, too. I hold my breath when somebody comes in.

A familiar voice says, "He ain't in here. Too bad."

"I told you that wasn't him. If it had of been, he'd of either turned around or else speeded up when you hollered. C'mon, Lonny, let's shoot some pool."

The door closes behind them, and I'm still perched in the stall, waiting for my heartbeat to slow down, when somebody comes in. I hear a lot of bathroom sounds, and then somebody *else* comes in. I'm wondering if I'm ever going to get out of here when the two guys start talking.

"Hey, did you hear what happened to Hawkins?"

"I've been wondering where he's been the last couple days."

"He's gone. They came for him in the night, and that was the last anybody's seen of him."

"*Who* came for him?"

"Security."

"What the heck had he done?"

"I heard he shot off his mouth about this place in some joint down in Santa Fe. People say all the bars and restaurants there have FBI men working as bartenders and waiters, and I guess it must be—"

Must be true, I think as the door thuds shut behind them. I let myself out of the stall and head for home, thinking about what I just heard, remembering what Dad said about secrecy being enforced. Boy, he sure knew what he was talking about.

But how could an ordinary GI like this Hawkins know about what's going on here? What could he have said about this place that made Security come for him in the night? And where is he now? I wonder about that all the way home.

Mom's already setting the table when I come in, and she looks up and says, "Hi, hon. No newspaper?"

The paper. "I—I guess I forgot. Sorry."

"Oh, well. Your father's news magazine came in today's mail, so he'll have something to read, and I was already planning to write to Vivian and Grandma."

"Tell them hi from me. And tell Viv I kind of like being an only child."

I go to my room, take the Secret Project notebook out of my desk drawer, and list Sam's name right after George's in the Personnel section. After I pencil in "Blue" under Badge Color for both of them, I flip a couple of pages and start a new category—RUMORS AND OBSERVATIONS. That's where I write down everything I found out today. I start with my conclusion that the scientists are working on some kind of explosive device, then jot down what I overheard in the PX bathroom. Last of all, I add: "Lots of orange badges at the Tech Area. Lots more blue badge scientists than white badge ones."

I hear Dad come in and wait till I figure he and Mom have finished their welcome-home hug before I turn off my light and head for the kitchen.

"Hi, Dad. Guess who I saw today? George Somebody—he was on the outing last Sunday."

"George Nast," Dad says. "One of our best young chemists."

Bingo! "He was with another guy who knows you. A young guy named Sam."

"Must have been Sam Solomon. He was a grad student in chemistry at the university a couple years ago."

Bingo again!

"Let your father get ready for dinner, Fritz," Mom says. "You can talk to him at the table."

Dad goes to wash up, and I dash back to my room to add George's and Sam's last names and "Chemist" to the chart in the Personnel section of my notebook. Not a bad day's work. Actually, it's been a pretty satisfactory day—Kathy didn't stop speaking to me because of my "real winners don't brag" remark, Manny and his friends saw that I'm not a complete dud at basketball, and Lonny and Red didn't get hold of me down at the PX.

"Dinner, Fritz!" Mom calls from the kitchen, and I head for the table, thinking that "Fritz" has a lot better life here on the Hill than "Franklin" did back in Indiana.

Chapter Six

Kathy's waiting for me when I leave to go back to school after lunch. "I keep forgetting to give you this," she says, handing me a piece of paper. "It's for your notebook—the information on the scientists in our building."

"This is great, Kathy, I tell her when I see Chemist, White Badge neatly enclosed in parentheses by the top two names and Metallurgist, Blue Badge by the bottom one. Wondering what a metallurgist does, I fold the paper and put it in my pocket.

Kathy gives me a funny look and says, "I still don't understand why you're making this list."

I can't believe she doesn't get it. "For the same reason I'm identifying the plants and animals I see out here and listing them in my Flora and Fauna notebook."

Kathy thinks that over for a minute and says, "You mean 'because it's there'?"

"Yeah. It's a challenge. What about you? How come you're helping me?"

"Because I hate this place and all its secrets!" Kathy bursts out.

I actually feel my mouth falling open. "You hate it here? But why?"

She ticks off the reasons on her fingers. "No bath-tub, no telephone, no sidewalks to roller-skate on.

There's dust everywhere—except when there's mud. And all the rules! I can't leave here to visit my grandma, and she can't come here to visit, either. I can't even write to my best friend back home."

"How come you can't write to her? My mom is always sending letters to my sister."

Kathy gives me an exasperated look. "I could *write* to her, but I couldn't *say* anything."

"I don't get it."

She sighs. "Every letter that goes out of here is read by the censors, okay?" I nod, and she says, "Well, anything I wouldn't mind a censor reading isn't worth saying. Not to a best friend, anyway."

"Oh." I still don't get it, but what the heck. "My mom had a letter returned by the censors because she complained about all the dust—as if that would tell the enemy where this mesa is and what's going on up here."

"Doesn't something like that make you hate this place even more, Fritz? I don't think I could stand living here if I didn't know my dad's working to help our side beat the Germans to some really important discovery that's going to end the war."

Bingo! Bingo! Bingo! No wonder everything's so secret. "You think they're working on something like those V-1 and V-2 rockets the Germans are using against England?"

Kathy frowns. "Gosh, I never even thought about what exactly they're doing. All I know is, my dad's always at the Lab. I hardly ever see him except on Sundays, which is another thing I hate about this place."

"My dad goes back to work every night after dinner, but that doesn't keep me from liking it here. I like everything about this place—except for that welcoming committee up ahead." My heart beats a little faster.

"We ought to start coming to school later," Kathy says.

"I guess we could, but it seems sort of cowardly."

Kathy gives me a wise look and quotes, "'He who fights and runs away, lives to fight another day.'"

Fights? I sure hope it never comes to that, 'cause the only fight I could win is a battle of wits. I did fine with the punching bag Dad got me, but I knew it wasn't going to hit me back. "How about if I pretend to tie my shoe or something? Wait up." I retie both my sneakers, managing to delay us enough that the bell is ringing by the time we reach the edge of the school yard.

Mrs. James is writing something on the board when we slip into our seats, and I concentrate on looking like I've been sitting here all along. She turns around and asks, "Do I have a volunteer to solve this equation for the class?"

I'm about to raise my hand when Manny says, "I'll give it a try." He slouches to the board and picks up a piece of chalk. A couple of the girls titter, and Mrs. James frowns—at Manny! From the look on her face, you'd think she's worried that he's going to scrawl obscenities all over her blackboard.

But instead, he starts to work the problem, writing out each step the way I've showed him in those after-school sessions. When he finishes, he stands there for another couple of seconds, and I know he's checking his work before he moves aside so Mrs. James can see what he's done.

"Very good, Manny," she says, and you've got to give her credit, 'cause she somehow manages not to sound surprised.

When Manny and I meet in the library after school, I tell him, "You did great in math class today."

He tries not to look pleased. "Heck, that problem she put up was exactly like the ones we had for homework last night." He lowers his voice and says, "Listen, Fritz. If Lonny and his pal give you any trouble, you let me know. Okay?"

Uh-oh. "More trouble than usual, you mean?"

Manny shrugs and opens his math book. "You just remember what I've told you."

"I guess that's fair enough, since you obviously remember what I've told you. About math," I add when he gives me a puzzled look.

44

Chapter Seven

I climb onto the army bus that's taking people over to the pueblo to attend the feast day celebration and slide into an empty seat near the front. I'm feeling sort of conspicuous, since the other passengers all seem to be with somebody, so I'm glad when Kathy plunks down beside me.

"How come you didn't tell me you were going tonight?" she asks, and without waiting for an answer, she points to the composition book on my lap and says, "Don't tell me you're planning on doing your homework on the bus, Fritz."

"Heck, no. This is for taking notes." I hand her Notes on Modern American Indians and say, "You can look at it, if you want."

She thumbs through the pages and stops at the one headed "Native Crafts Sold on the Plaza at Santa Fe, 1944." I watch her run a finger down the list I made. It's a fairly detailed list, complete with subheadings—jewelry, weaving, pottery—and descriptions. "I took the army bus to Santa Fe last Saturday and poked around for a while," I explain.

"Santa Fe's a pokey place," Kathy says. "In my opinion, they shouldn't even call it a city." She closes the notebook and starts to hand it back.

"Wait a minute. You haven't seen the map I'm making to show the Indian villages." I find it and point out the X's marking three of the pueblos, including the one we're headed toward right now.

"What's all this for, anyway?" Kathy asks.

For? "It's—well, it's sort of a collection. This is the third notebook I've started since we came here, and I've got a bunch of blank ones in my desk drawer just waiting for my next idea. I'm collecting rocks, too," I tell her, "and— Hey, we're here already."

Kathy stands up, and I notice she's got this glazed look in her eyes. I guess I got sort of carried away, telling her all that stuff. "Sorry if I've been a bore."

"You're more like some kind of mad genius."

I don't know what to say to that, so I just lead the way off the bus. "Come on," I tell her. "Our maid invited me to sit with her family, but she won't mind if you come, too."

"Actually, I'm supposed to sit with *our* maid, but I don't see her. Oh, wait—there she is."

"Juanita works for your family, too? Swell!" I barrel my way through the crowd toward her, and Kathy stays right behind me. Pretty soon we're sitting up on the flat roof of Juanita's adobe house, and she's introduced us to a lot of other people I figure must be her relatives.

Some of the families from the Hill are sitting on their maids' roofs, too, but most visitors are finding places to sit a little way back from the bonfire in the middle of this open square—I guess they'd call it a plaza—and you can sense the crowd's excitement. The expectation.

I open Notes on Modern American Indians to a fresh page and hand Kathy the flashlight I brought along. "Hold this for me," I tell her, and she shines it on the page while I make a rough diagram of the plaza and the adobe buildings that surround it. Very rough, 'cause I'm no artist.

Pretty soon we hear drums, and everybody quiets down as this procession comes weaving along, casting long shadows in the firelight, chanting and dancing. Kathy clicks off the flashlight, and when I whisper, "Hey, turn that back on," she ignores me. Guess I'll have to make mental notes.

We watch the costumed dancers with their feathered headdresses, and Juanita tries to explain what's going on. I don't understand everything she says, but from what I read at the library today, I'm pretty sure it all has something to do with her religion. And I'm very sure there's not a chance I'm going to forget a single thing before I have a chance to write it all down.

It's late when I get home, but Mom and Dad are still up, sitting in front of the fire, eating popcorn. I take a handful and tell them all about the festival. When I'm through, Mom reminds me that it's a school night, and I take another handful of popcorn and say, "I don't know how you expect me to sleep with that racket going on downstairs."

"That racket, as you call it, happens to be a Beethoven symphony," Mom says, and then she turns to Dad. "Which reminds me, Verne. One of the women at work told me her husband always plays records when they're in the living room and turns on the radio when they're in the kitchen or the bedroom to cover their conversations. He's worried that Security might have hidden microphones in their apartment. How likely do you think that is?"

I hold my breath and wait for Dad to answer. "It's certainly a possibility," he says. "One of my young colleagues was called on the carpet for talking to his wife about his work, and there's no other way anyone could have known."

Holy cow! "But how could Security hide the microphones without anybody knowing? Wouldn't the neighbors be suspicious?"

Mom says, "People are in and out of these apartments all the time—maintenance men, maids, electricians. It would be easy enough. That faucet in the kitchen sink doesn't leak anymore even though I never got around to reporting it."

In spite of the fire crackling in the fireplace, I suddenly feel icy cold. "You mean Security might be listening in on us right now?"

"I doubt it, son," Dad says, "but if anyone ever does listen in on us, it won't matter, because I never discuss anything about my work." He looks at his watch, and I take the hint.

"Good night, you two," I say, and then I raise my voice a little and say, "Good night, Security."

Back in my room I find Notes on the Secret Project and open it to Rumors and Observations. My hand shakes a little as I write: "There is evidence that Security has hidden microphones in the apartments of at least some scientists to make sure they aren't talking to their wives about the project. One scientist is known to have been caught doing this."

I'm putting the notebook back in my desk drawer when I have a terrible thought. What if somebody from Security comes snooping around our apartment and finds this?

My heart begins to race, and I glance around, looking for a better place to keep the notebook. To hide it. The problem is, no matter where I put it, whenever I'm not home, I'll worry that somebody might be prowling through the apartment, looking for something suspicious. It makes as much sense as hiding microphones and listening in on people's conversations.

There's only one thing to do. I'm going to have to keep that notebook with me all the time. But what if I lose it? Set it down someplace and go off without it? My knapsack—that's the answer. I'll keep the notebook in my knapsack, and I'll wear the knapsack everywhere I go.

Trouble is, everybody's going to think it's really strange to wear a knapsack and never take it off. But I guess I'd rather be "That crazy kid with the knapsack" than "That poor kid Lonny and Red have it in for."

I fish my knapsack out of the closet where I tossed it after Sunday's outing and put all my notebooks in it plus my guidebooks, so if Mom or Dad ask any questions I can say I'm keeping everything at my fingertips. What the heck—might as well put in my school books, too.

It isn't till I'm finally in bed that I realize that I didn't write anything about the festival at the pueblo in my Modern American Indians notebook.

I'm already at the breakfast table when Dad comes in and says, "I see your knapsack there by the door, son. I hope this doesn't mean you're running away from home."

If you didn't know him, you'd swear he was serious. "Guess I'm going to have to stay here on the

49

Hill," I tell him, "'cause by the time I packed all my books and notebooks, there wasn't any room left for a change of clothes and some food."

"Glad to hear you're staying, son," he says, pouring milk into his coffee.

I'm halfway through my cereal when Mom says, "Are you all right, Fritz? You're awfully quiet this morning."

"I keep thinking about our unseen audience, if you know what I mean," I tell her. "You know—Security."

Dad says, "My guess is that any listening devices in apartments would only be monitored in the evening. Most people are so rushed in the morning they aren't likely to be giving away secrets, and Security wouldn't have any reason to listen in when the scientists are at work."

Boy, that makes me feel a lot better. If I always keep my Secret Project notebook with me, maybe I won't have to worry about Security after all. Which means I can concentrate on worrying about what Lonny and Red are going to do next.

When I leave for school, Kathy's waiting at the foot of the steps. "You look like you're ready for a hike," she says. "How come you've got that knapsack on?"

"It's a great way to carry your books and stuff, Kathy."

"Nobody carries their school things in a knapsack, Fritz. I think you're just trying to be different."

She's wrong. I don't have to try—being different comes naturally to me.

When I don't answer, Kathy says, "Well, you're really asking for it, 'cause when Lonny and Red see you wearing that stupid knapsack, they're going to

50

laugh their heads off. And when they're through laughing, they'll snatch it right off your back and dump everything out on the ground."

I stop short. "But my notebooks are in there! What if they get hold of Notes on the Secret Project?"

Kathy stops, too, and for a couple of seconds we stare at each other. And then she says, "Quick—turn around. I'll carry the notebooks for you."

She gets them out, and I watch her stack her books on top of them. "Come on," she says. "We'd better hurry."

The guys are over on the side of the schoolyard, and as they come toward us, Red calls, "Hey, Fritz! What's that you got on your back, a papoose?"

A couple of other kids laugh, but I pretend not to notice. "Come here and I'll show you," I call back to them, shrugging off the knapsack. By the time I undo the buckles and open the flap, the two of them and a bunch of other kids have come over, and I say, "Look at all the stuff I've managed to fit inside here—a couple of library books, the three-ring binder I keep class notes in, and all my school books. See? Science, math, literature—"

I start pulling them out, one at a time, but Lonny says, "We got better things to do than look at school books, Fritz."

"Especially *your* school books," Red adds.

"I still say you guys ought to try carrying your stuff in a knapsack, because—"

The bell sounds, and the curious group that had gathered around us starts toward the door, with Lonny and Red in the lead. I load the books back into my knapsack, and Kathy hands me my notebooks.

Neither one of us says anything as we hurry toward the building, but I'm pretty sure Kathy knows as well as I do that I don't have to worry anymore about having my knapsack snatched and dumped out.

Chapter Eight

It's pretty late when I leave for school, so I'm surprised to find Kathy standing at the foot of the stairs leading from our balcony. I try to walk down the steps naturally and not let on how sore my leg muscles are after hiking to the top of that mountain on yesterday's outing.

"It's about time," Kathy says, and before I can remind her that I never asked her to wait, she's talking at me. "I've decided you ought to start another notebook."

She's decided! "A notebook on what?"

"On what it was like for Jewish kids in Germany when Hitler came into power. This woman I walked with on the hike yesterday—her name's Helga—was in high school then, and she was telling me."

Frankly, that's not my idea of notebook material, but it sounds interesting. A lot more interesting than hearing for the tenth time how worried Kathy is 'cause they haven't had a letter from her brother overseas for almost a month. "So what kind of things did Helga tell you?"

"Well, first of all, the other kids at school turned against her because she was Jewish—her best friend actually stopped speaking to her! And then her father lost his job because Jews weren't allowed to work for the government any longer, so her family went to

Sweden. But her favorite cousins stayed in Germany, and she heard from them how things kept getting worse and worse. Can you believe that Jewish kids couldn't go to school with other Germans? Or that Jews weren't allowed to have radios? Weren't allowed to ride the trains and buses?"

Kathy's sounding more and more upset, and when I glance over at her, I see that she looks upset, too. "I never knew about all that," I tell her, figuring I ought to say something. "Maybe I will start another notebook."

"You know what really worries me, Fritz? Ever since Helga told me all that, I'm really worried that Germany might win the war and then the Nazis would come over here and—"

"That's why our fathers came here to work in the Lab, Kath. To make sure the Germans don't win the war," I remind her. The bell rings before she can answer, and we both run toward the building. We're the last ones in, but that's okay with me. I'd rather be at the end of the line than up front with Lonny and Red.

Fourth period, Mrs. Jackson sends a few of us at a time to the library to use the reference books for a report she's assigned, and I end up going at the same time as Manny and Kathy. Manny gets right to work, copying something out of an encyclopedia, but Kathy buttonholes me and asks, "So are you going to do it?"

"Do what?"

She rolls her eyes. "Start that new notebook. The one about being Jewish and growing up in Germany, like Helga and her cousin."

Dad says sometimes the best defense is a good offense, so I try it. "Speaking of Helga, how come you hiked with her the whole time yesterday? I thought we agreed to try and listen in on what the scientists were saying."

"For your information, Helga *is* one of the scientists. She's a physicist with a blue badge."

"You're kidding! A woman physicist?"

Kathy nods. "She got her inspiration from reading about some famous woman scientist in Berlin. Helga said if it hadn't been for the work that woman did after she fled to Sweden—she was Jewish, too—this Lab might not even exist."

One of the tenth grade girls looks up from her book to frown at us, so I whisper, "Come on, Kath, let's go over by the encyclopedias." I pick one at random and pretend to be showing her something in it while I say, "So how come you kept trying to get me to start a new notebook instead of telling me Helga was a physicist with a blue badge?"

Kathy looks embarrassed. "I guess I forgot. All those things she told me were a lot more interesting than names and badge colors."

She's right about that. I make a split-second decision and say, "What's really interesting are the rumors and observations I've been collecting about the secret project. After school, I'll let you read that part of my notebook."

"Listen, Fritz, if we're going to be partners, I'm going to read the whole thing. Hand it over."

"Now? But—"

"Now, Fritz." She holds out her hand.

Who said we were partners, anyway? Wishing I'd kept my mouth shut, I slip off my knapsack and get out the notebook, then lead the way to the table that's sort of private but not so far away from Manny that he'll think we're avoiding him. I sit opposite Kathy while she scans the divider tabs and zeroes in on Rumors and Observations.

She flips to that section and reads all the entries. Then she slides the notebook across the table and says, "You'd better put this away. I'll read the rest of it at lunchtime. We can sit on your steps, in case your dad's wrong about those microphones being turned off during the day."

Once I've got the notebook safely in my knapsack and have the straps buckled, Kathy whispers, "I don't blame you for keeping that notebook with you wherever you go. At first I thought you were—well, *eccentric*, but I don't think so anymore."

She was about to say "crazy." She used to think I was crazy. But before I can feel too bad about that, I realize something a lot more important: Even though she thought I was crazy, Kathy still wanted to be friends.

At lunchtime we sit part way up the balcony stairs while Kathy looks at the rest of my notebook entries. She flips to Personnel and glances at my list, then takes the pencil I keep clipped to the cover and writes: "Helga Gottlieb, Physicist, Blue Badge." I decide not to mention that it's pretty dumb to write "blue *badge*" in the column headed "*Badge* Color."

Now Kathy's looking at the code words. "I've heard a couple of these when Dad has friends over," she says. "Like 'the Gadget.' But I never heard this last one—'tickling the dragon's tail.' That's got to mean something really dangerous. Did you hear it on the hike yesterday?"

I shake my head. "Mom invited a couple of the bachelor scientists over for a home-cooked meal night before last, and—"

"Did they actually sit there at the table and talk in code right in front of you and your mother? After she'd cooked dinner for them?"

"Let me finish, will you? I listened through the wall. After I helped Mom with the dishes, she said we should stay in our rooms so the men could talk about their work."

Kathy says, "I guess they figured that since they were talking in code they didn't have to worry about keeping their voices down."

"Actually, I tried a trick I'd read about. See, if you take a drinking glass and put the bottom against the wall and press the rim to the side of your head so your ear's inside the glass, you can hear what's going on in the next room."

Kathy's eye are wide. "Where'd you read that?"

"In a book I got from the library. 'Course, it doesn't hurt that the walls of these apartments are pretty thin." I see our next door neighbor heading toward us with a sack of groceries, so I shove the notebook in my knapsack and carry the stuff upstairs for her.

When I come back to where Kathy's waiting for me, she says, "How come you never showed me that notebook before?"

"You never asked."

She rolls her eyes and says, "You'll have to do better than that, Fritz."

"I didn't think you'd be interested. Nobody's ever been interested in my notebooks—or my collections, either." Nobody my age, anyhow. Nobody but Dad.

"Well, *I'm* interested. Okay?"

"Okay, Kath. See you after lunch."

Kathy heads for home, and I'm about to go upstairs when Timmy sticks his head out of his apartment and singsongs gleefully, "Fritz has a girlfriend! Fritz has a girlfriend!"

Great. First Lonny and Red, and now Timmy.

"Fritz and Kath-y, up in a tree, k-i-s-s-i-n-g," he sings out. Something he learned from those first-graders in the next building, I guess.

"Look, squirt," I tell him, "She's a girl, and she's my friend, but she's not my girlfriend. I guess you're too young to understand that, though."

Timmy stomps his foot and says, "I am not too young!"

"Not too young for what?" I ask him.

"Not too young to understand that Kathy isn't your girlfriend." Timmy sticks his tongue out at me and ducks back inside, pulling the door shut behind him, and I head up the steps to our apartment, feeling pretty good. I think I'm going to like having a partner to help me with my Notes on the Secret Project.

Chapter Nine

Lonny has pretty much left me alone lately, but when I see him and Red hanging around outside the PX, I know who they're waiting for. Sure enough, soon as they see me coming, Lonny plants himself right smack between me and the door.

"Hey. You been helping Manny with his math homework after school."

"Yeah. So?" Dad says it's important not to let guys like these think you're scared of them.

"Well, I want some help, too."

I frown and pretend to be thinking about it. "Maybe when Manny's all caught up I can—"

Lonny shakes his head. "There ain't no 'maybe' about this, Fritz. Beginning now, I'm gonna give you my math workbook every day after school. You'll do the assignment and give it back to me the next morning."

"If you think I'm going to do your homework for you, you're crazy." The words just sort of burst out and surprise me as much as they do Lonny. He narrows his eyes and takes a step toward me, and I automatically back up. But Red's moved behind me, and he grabs my arm and twists it, holding me against him. I know he'll twist even harder if I make any effort to break away, so I clench my teeth and try not to let on how much he's hurting me. A bunch of enlisted men walk past and don't even glance at us.

Lonny's really enjoying this. "Now, about doing my homework—" He pauses, like he's waiting for me to agree, and when I don't, Red gives my arm another twist, bending it up and forcing my shoulder downward.

I clench my teeth and say, "My dad's waiting for his newspaper, you know." I think of adding that he's six-foot four and weighs 250 pounds and he's likely to come storming down here any minute to find out why I'm not home yet. But like Kathy says, I'm not a very good liar.

"So go in and get it for him, Fritzy-Witzy. But take my math workbook with you." Lonny holds it out to me and says, "Do the next page and give it back to me in the morning. Okay?"

That last word is definitely meant as a threat, but I don't answer him till Red gives my arm a twist that hurts all the way from my shoulder to my fingertips.

"Okay!" It comes out half gasp, half squeak, and Red releases me, giving me enough of a shove that I wind up staring at Lonny's chin. It's not my fault if I mean *"Okay, I'll go in and get the newspaper"* and Lonny thinks I mean *"Okay, I'll do the math homework for you."* I let him stand there holding out his workbook while I get my knapsack unfastened and open the flap, and then I take it from him.

I manage not to rub my sore arm until I'm inside the PX. My heartbeat slows to normal while I'm waiting in line to pay for the paper, and when I come outside again, those goons are gone. All the way home, I try to figure out what to do. I'm sure of two things: (1) If I know what's good for me, I'll do Lonny's homework for him, and (2) I'm not going to do Lonny's homework for him. My stomach starts to knot up when I remember the menacing tone of his voice when he said, "There ain't no maybe about this, Fritz." I rub my aching arm again and try not to think about what Lonny might have in store for me tomorrow.

The minute I open the door to our apartment, the warmth and the spicy aroma coming from the kitchen tell me that Mom's fixed my favorite dinner—meat loaf and baked potatoes—and I hope I can do it justice.

"Smells good, Mom. What's the occasion?"

"No occasion. I just got tired of cooking on that hot plate and decided to fix an honest-to-goodness meal for a change," she says. "I had enough ration stamps for steaks, but there weren't any left when I ran over to the commissary at lunchtime." She sets a steaming bowl on the table and says, "Wash up, Fritz. You know your father needs to get back to the Lab."

"Sorry I'm late." I hang up my jacket and wash at the sink before I slide into my place at the table. I'm at least a yard from the big old coal stove some army genius decided to make standard equipment for kitchens here on the Hill, but I can feel it's heat. I hope Mom goes back to using the electric hot plate tomorrow night. Assuming I'll still be around after Lonny and Red get through with me.

Dad passes me my plate, and I see that today's green vegetable is canned peas. Today's olive-green vegetable would be more accurate. I stare down at my plate, trying not to think about facing those goons tomorrow.

"Is something wrong with the meat loaf, Fritz?"

Mom's unspoken "that-I-rushed-home-from-work-and-slaved-over-a-hot-stove-to-make-just-for-you" hangs in the air, and I know I'd better forget everything except showing enthusiasm for dinner. "I'm just appreciating the tempting aroma before I dig in," I tell her as I pick up my fork.

She gives me a long look and asks, "Did something go wrong at school today?"

"School was fine, Mom." Just don't ask me about after school.

From the other end of the table, Dad says, "How is your math student coming along, Fritz?"

"I guess whoever put him in that class because he had 'po-TEN-tial' knew what they were doing, 'cause he's coming along really well. Some of his friends seem to resent it, though," I add, forking up the meat loaf.

Mom frowns. "It's hard to imagine the children of scientists having that kind of attitude."

"These aren't scientists' kids," I tell her. "They're guys who live over in the Quonset huts like Manny does or else in the trailer camp. They act like he's putting on airs or something because he's in pre-algebra instead of the basic math class." I try not to think about the basic math workbook in my knapsack. Lonny's notebook.

"Do any of the kids resent you because you do well in school?" Dad asks.

I look across the table and meet his eyes. "Not really."

He raises one eyebrow at me the way he does and repeats my words as a question. "Not really?"

"Lots of other kids do well in school, so it's not that. It's got to be something else about me. Something about the way I am."

"I think the way you are is just fine, son," Dad says. "More meat loaf?"

I shake my head. In a way, what he said makes me feel better, but it makes me feel worse, too, because now I know for sure that I can't take the easy way out and do Lonny's homework for him.

Chapter Ten

I glance at my watch and walk a little faster. I hate standing Kathy up like this, but if my plan's going to work, I've got to meet Lonny and Red before school, and I couldn't wait for her any longer. Too bad Timmy wasn't playing outside this morning so he could tell Kath I had to leave early.

Strange that when I make some friends for the first time in my life, one of them's a girl and the other's a Spanish-American kid who's never been farther from the mesa than Santa Fe. I wonder—

Uh-oh. Lonny and Red are already waiting for me at the edge of the schoolyard. I take a deep breath and concentrate on striding confidently toward them. Before either one can say anything, I call, "I haven't done your math homework yet, but there's still lunch hour."

"Hey, that means I won't have time to copy the answers," Red complains.

Lonny grabs a handful of my jacket front and hauls me toward him. "From now on, you'll do my homework before you start on yours, you understand?"

"Yeah." I manage to look him in the eye.

"Then say it."

"I understand that you want me to do your home-work before I start on mine."

For a second, I think Lonny might be going to

spit on me or something, the way he's looking at me, but he only says, "You have that work finished and back here after lunch, or else." And then he gives me a shove that almost knocks me off my feet.

The two of them walk away without looking back, and I stand here breathing hard, glaring at their backs. I could save myself a heck of a lot of trouble if I knuckled under and did that homework. A page of basic math wouldn't take me long, and then maybe they'd lay off me. Nah, they wouldn't do that. Before I knew it, they'd be after me to write their book reports or something.

I'm brooding about what I'm letting myself in for when I see this new kid standing near the flagpole. He's a lot taller than me, thin with dark hair, and from the way he's dressed, I have a hunch he's foreign.

He turns and looks at me, like he felt my eyes on him, so I make myself walk over and say, "Hi, you're new, aren't you?"

He nods and gives a little bow. "I am Jacob," he says. "My parents and I arrived here only yesterday."

"I'm Fritz, and I got here the day before school started. What grade are you in?"

Jacob frowns. "I do not know how your 'grades' are, but I have just had my fourteenth birthday."

"Well, I'm twelve-and-a-half, and I'm in the combined seventh-eighth grade class, so you'll probably be in ninth. Where are you from?"

"Germany, originally, but my family moved to Denmark after Hitler came into power. More recently, we have lived in London." He says it like a speech he's memorized.

"You had to leave Germany because you're Jewish?"

I ask him. He looks surprised by my question, and I remember too late that for some reason it isn't considered polite to ask somebody about their religion.

Glancing away from me, he says, "We left Germany when Hitler forbade non-Aryans to hold scientific positions and my father could not work. And we left Denmark last year when word came that the Nazis planned to 'eliminate' the Jews who lived there."

Wow, maybe Kathy was right and I ought to start a new notebook. "Did the Germans—"

"Enough about me," Jacob says firmly. "Tell me now about where you have come from."

"I'm from Indiana—it's in the Midwest," I tell him, trying to hide my embarrassment. "My dad was a physics professor before we came here." I think of the Personnel section of Notes on the Secret Project and ask, "Is your father a physicist?"

Jacob nods, but before I can find out anything else, the bell sounds and the usual crowd starts to shove through the door. Jacob looks shocked, so I say, "Um, this is probably going to be a lot different from the other schools you've been to. Some of the kids are a pretty rough bunch."

"Why do the teachers not keep discipline?" Jacob asks. "How are we to learn?"

Instead of answering, I say, "Come on, we'd better go inside." Boy, between his good manners and the way he's dressed, like he's going to church or something, he's going to stick out like a sore thumb. I sure hope the kids give him half a chance.

On the way home at noon I tell Kathy, "Don't wait for me after lunch, okay?"

"How come you don't want to walk with me anymore?"

"It's not that, honest. It's just that I'm going back late, and if you wait for me, you'll be tardy."

Kathy says, "But what about the math test? Or are you such a whiz you don't need the whole period to finish it?"

The math test. "I forgot about the test. Guess I won't be going back late after all." Now what am I going to do?

"So how come you were going to go back late?" Kathy asks.

"Look, if I'd known you were going to give me the third degree, I'd have let you stand in the cold and wait for me."

"Like you did this morning?" she asks, and I can hear the resentment in her voice.

I feel my face turning red, and I'm about to apologize when suddenly Kathy says, "I'll bet not going back on time has something to do with Lonny and Red. Tell me, Fritz."

"There you go again, sounding like my mother." I mean it as a joke, but it comes out like a complaint. "If I tell you, do you promise not to say anything to Mrs. James? Or anybody?"

"I haven't said anything about your Notes on the Secret Project, have I?"

So I tell her how Lonny's trying to make me to do his math homework.

Kathy thinks a minute before she says, "If you go ahead and do it for him, maybe he and Red wouldn't be after you all the time."

"If that line of thinking worked, your brother would

be at college instead of overseas." Boy, that sure got her attention. "See, nobody stopped Hitler when he took over Austria and sort of gobbled up Czechoslovakia, so he went ahead and invaded Poland. That was when England and France declared—"

"*Okay*, Fritz, I get the picture. But Lonny is going to declare war on *you* if you don't do what he says."

She's right, but I'm still not going to do it.

I head for the apartment, wishing Manny wasn't absent today of all days. But I forget about everything else the minute I see Juanita sitting at our kitchen table.

"Come and eat Indian food," she says, and I see that she's fixed two plates.

"Hey, neat!" I sit down, and she points to each thing, saying its name—tamale, tortilla, and something I don't quite get. I taste that first and decide it must be some strange kind of vegetable that I'm going to have to eat so I don't hurt her feelings.

Since this seems like the perfect chance to collect some information for Notes on Modern American Indians, I ask, "Juanita, do you weave rugs?" She nods, and I ask if she makes pottery, too. Everything I ask her, she nods, so I start to wonder if maybe that's her way of being polite.

Oh, well. At least I've got some first-hand information about Indian food to write in my notebook. I do that as soon as Juanita leaves, and then I get out Notes on the Secret Project. Under Personnel, I write in "Jacob's Father" and "Physicist," and under Rumors and Observations, I add: "They're bringing in more scientists. I should have figured out they were going to, since they've been building more apartments." I'm still writing when somebody knocks at the door. Kathy. She waits for me to get my jacket and knapsack, and I figure she's making sure I leave on time. Or maybe she's showing moral support, or something. I guess that's part of being a friend.

Kathy doesn't say much on the way back to school, which is fine with me. But when we're almost to the school yard, she says, "There they are. Waiting for you."

"You got my workbook?" Lonny yells.

"Yeah. It's in my knapsack." I shrug it off and take my time undoing the straps and buckles that close it. Then I sort through my stuff a couple of times till I hear the bell. I hand over the workbook, and Lonny grabs it and runs toward the building.

Kathy gives me that funny look of hers and says, "You told me you weren't going to do his homework for him."

"I didn't. I just gave him back his workbook. Let's go."

We make it to our seats just as Mrs. James starts handing out the math test. It's hard, and I barely finish in time to check over my answers and change a 51 to a 15. Kathy was right—I needed the whole period. It's a good thing I didn't come in late, like I was planning to.

I keep an eye out for Lonny and Red in the hall between my afternoon classes, but I don't even catch a glimpse of them. And now that school's out for the day, I figure I'm safe, 'cause Mrs. James is sure to make them stay late and do that homework assignment.

But I'm wrong—they're waiting for me by the outside door. My mouth goes dry and I cross my fingers, hoping my emergency plan works, 'cause it's a huge gamble. I take a deep breath and tell myself to act confident.

"How come you guys are leaving?" I call as I force myself to walk toward them. "Don't you know the principal wants to see the two of you right away?"

The snake-mean looks on their faces change to something like dread, and I add, "You'd better hurry."

I walk on past them, but once I'm out the door, I take off running. My knapsack bounces against my back as I dash across the schoolyard and head for home. This is probably the farthest I ever ran, and I know it's the fastest. My chest feels like I've been stabbed or something, and I wonder if kids ever get heart attacks. I burst into the apartment, slam the door shut, and lean against it.

I'm still struggling to catch my breath when Mom comes out of the bedroom. She looks tousled and bleary-eyed, but she wakes up fast when she sees the state I'm in. "What's happened? Are you all right?" I give a jerky nod, and she leads me into the kitchen and sort of pushes me into my chair.

Mom brings me a glass of water and watches while I gulp it down. "Okay, Fritz," she says, sitting down at the table opposite me. "Talk."

"Sure, Mom. How come you're home so early? You have another bad headache?"

Ignoring my questions, she says, "I want to know why you came running home like somebody was after you." She leans forward and asks, "*Was* somebody after you?"

I don't want to tell her, but I know I'm going to. "Well, you see, there's this kid at school, and—" The next thing I know, I'm sobbing out the whole story, and whenever I stop to take a breath, Mom says, "And what else?" until there's nothing more left to tell.

When she figures she's heard it all, she says, "Tomorrow morning I'm going over to that school and—"

"You *can't!* I'd never live it down."

She glares at me and says, "Do you have a better idea? I refuse to have my son terrorized by a bully."

"What's this about a bully?" Dad asks from the kitchen doorway. I never even heard him come home.

Mom gives Dad a hug, but you can tell her heart's not in it. "Tell your father what you told me, Fritz," she says, pulling away. "I've got to start supper."

So I tell the whole story again while Dad listens, and this time I don't bawl about it. When I finish, Mom says, "I think one of us should march over to that school first thing in the morning, but your son seems to object to that idea."

Dad runs his fingers through his hair and says, "Well, kiddo, do you have a better suggestion? Those two are really going to have it in for you now that it's obvious you won't do their homework for them. They're going to have to make good on their threats, and I don't think any of us want to see that happen."

"Manny—he's the kid I'm helping with math—said if Lonny gives me any trouble, I should let him know about it. I could do that." Provided he isn't absent again.

Mom makes an impatient *tsk* sound, and Dad asks, "How do you think that would help, son?"

"Manny outweighs Lonny. He's tougher, too," I add, remembering the look that came over Lonny's face when I told him and Red the principal wanted to see them.

Dad thinks that over for a minute before he says,

"All right, we'll try it your way first. But if the situation doesn't improve, I'm going to have to step in."

"Okay, Dad." At least that wouldn't be as humiliating as having Mom show up at the school.

Chapter Eleven

Instead of the brilliant sunlight I've come to expect here on the Hill, the sky is gray and gloomy this morning. Coming out of the apartment is sort of like walking into an untinted photograph, except for Kathy's red jacket. She's waiting for me at the bottom of the steps, and I figure she's going to ask what happened with the goons after school yesterday. But she doesn't.

"Did you finish that math test?" she asks.

"Sure. Had enough time left to check over my answers. How about you?"

Kathy gets this glum look on her face and says, "I almost didn't finish. Before *you* came here, *I* was always the one with the best grades in math."

Uh-oh. "Speaking of math, I've got to tell you what happened after school yesterday. Lonny and Red are really going to have it in for me now." Kathy listens to the whole story, and when I finish, her forehead creases into a frown. "Aren't you scared, Fritz?"

She can always tell when I'm lying, so I might as well admit it. "Yeah. I'm counting on Manny being there to stick up for me."

"I'll go on ahead and look for him," Kathy says, and she's running toward the school before I can stop her. Not that I really want to. Boy, it's bad enough to have to be rescued by Manny—but by Kathy, too?

A bunch of little kids go tearing past, and I won-

73

der if maybe it's later than I'd thought. But when I get in sight of the schoolyard, I see that nobody's started to go in yet. And then I see Lonny and Red heading for me.

Don't let them know you're afraid. "Hey, aren't you two going the wrong way?" They scowl and keep right on coming. *He who fights and runs away lives to fight another day.* And so does he who runs away without fighting at all.

I light off for the middle of the schoolyard, zigzagging between a couple groups of kids, thinking maybe I can keep ahead of these guys till Manny shows up. Figuring that if I can't, they aren't going to beat me up in front of everybody.

But I'm wrong. One of them grabs my knapsack and yells, "I've got him!" I'd slip right out of the straps if my notebooks weren't in that knapsack, but—

I feel a mighty shove and hit the ground with such force I hardly know what's happened. Somebody yells "Fight!" and I hear the word passed along, sense that a curious circle is starting to form around us.

Instinctively, I use my arms and hands to protect my head, but somehow the two of them manage to turn me over. I try to get up, and they knock me down again. I roll over and scramble to my feet, but before I can run, Red grabs me from behind and holds my arms to my sides while Lonny takes a swing at me.

I rear back as far as I can, and the blow glances off the side of my face. The next one is a punch in the kisser, and after that I lose track. I'm thinking they might actually kill me when suddenly I'm not being beat on anymore. I sort of sink to the ground, not sure what's happened. Just hurting something awful and relieved that it's over.

The kids in the circle are chanting even louder now, so *somebody's* obviously being beat on. I manage to sit up, and I see Lonny and Red trying to defend themselves against another boy—that new kid, Jacob! Accompanied by the rhythmic chant of "Fight! Fight! Fight!" in the background, Jacob is punching and slugging like some kind of madman.

Finally a bunch of twelfth graders pull him off and hold onto him while Lonny and Red stagger away. "Man, what got into you, anyway?" one of the older guys asks Jacob.

Jacob wrenches himself out of their hold, and when he faces them, his body tense and his hands in fists, a couple of the guys take a step back. "How could you allow this to happen?" Jacob says, his voice shaking. "How could you allow this unfair two-against-one? How could you stand by and watch? Watch and do nothing to stop the unfairness? Watch and *enjoy* the unfairness?"

With each question, his voice gets louder and is pitched a little higher, and by the time he finally stops, the kids have all slunk off.

My lips feel like raw hamburger and probably look worse, but my teeth still seem to be in place. I struggle to my feet and straighten my knapsack, and when I turn to thank Jacob for coming to my rescue, he's walking away. His head's bowed, and his shoulders shake like he's sobbing, but he's not making a sound. I don't know what to do.

The bell must have rung, because now Mrs. Jackson's hurrying toward us across the empty schoolyard. I steal another look at Jacob, and then go to meet her.

"Oh, Fritz, your poor face! Kathy told me there was a fight out here, but I had no idea *you* were involved."

She sounds so incredulous I'd laugh if my face didn't hurt so much. "Actually, I was the one being fought."

Shading her eyes with her hand, she says, "Isn't that the new boy over there? Jacob? Was *he* fighting you?"

"He was fighting the kids who were fighting me. It's pretty complicated."

Mrs. Jackson straightens her shoulders and says sternly, "Complicated or not, we can't have you boys fighting, Fritz. Just look at you!"

If I look half as bad as I feel, I'm a sight. "Is it okay if I go home and get cleaned up?"

"That sounds like a very good idea. Hold some ice on your poor face."

I head for home, wondering what Mrs. Jackson is going to say to Jacob—and wondering about Jacob, too.

When Mom comes home from work and sees my black eye and fat lip she gets really upset—at *me.* "I don't know why I listened to you and your father. Where was this Manny who was supposed to be looking out for you?"

"In the library, trying to catch up on some of the work he missed when he was absent. Kathy told me when she stopped by after school with my assignments."

"That settles it, young man. First thing tomorrow morning, I'm going over to that school and—"

"Mom. MOM!" When I finally get her attention, I tell her about how the fight ended, about how Jacob rescued me.

Just as I finish, Dad comes in. When he sees my face, his jaw tightens, but he just sits down at the table with us and says, "Tell me what happened, son."

So I do, and when I finish, Dad says, "I'm sorry you had to take such a pounding, but I doubt that Lonny and Red or anyone else is going to bother you after this."

"And I'll bet nobody will dare bother Jacob. You should have seen him, Dad—he changed from this really polite, sort of brainy-looking kid into some kind of fighting machine. And then the way he lit into the kids who were watching—it was really something!"

"He sounds like a very troubled boy," Mom says.

Dad says quietly, "If you had been through what he has, you'd be troubled, too, Mona."

"You know Jacob?" I ask, surprised.

"I've met his father, Hermann Schwartz. He told me a little about life under the Nazis—including the painful discovery that his countrymen would stand by and allow their fellow citizens to be persecuted."

That must be what set Jacob off. He even used almost the same words, accusing the kids of standing by and watching the unfairness. Enjoying it. "You think Jacob's family was persecuted?"

"They probably wouldn't be alive today if Hermann hadn't been a scientist," Dad says.

"I don't get it."

Dad sighs. "Many of the Jews who tried to leave Europe in the 1930s couldn't find a country to accept them. But scientists like Hermann were welcomed with open arms pretty much anywhere they chose to go."

"Wait a minute," I say. "What's this about countries 'not accepting' the Jews?"

Dad sighs again. "Most countries have limits on immigration, on how many people may come in each year. Between that and prejudice against—"

"Let's talk about something else, shall we?" Mom says.

Very quietly, Dad says, "A word to the wise, son. If your mother doesn't want to talk about this, do you think your friend Jacob is going to want you asking him questions?"

I shake my head. I *know* he doesn't. He made that pretty clear yesterday.

I wait till Mom and Dad are both at the breakfast table before I make my entrance. In a fake announcer's voice, I say, "And here, in living color, we have young Fritz Madden."

Dad says, "In *livid* color would be more like it."

"Oh, dear. Your lip is starting to bleed again," Mom says. "You'd better stay home today, hon."

Dad shakes his head. "He has to go, Mona." He turns to me and says, "If Lonny and Red are at school and you're absent, they'll think they came out on top. But if you're there, they'll know that you can't be beaten down."

"And everybody will think I've got guts, right?"

Before Dad can answer, Mom makes that *tsk* sound and says, "Really, Fritz. Not at the breakfast table." But I know that's what Dad meant.

Kathy's waiting at the foot of the steps when I leave for school, and her eyes widen when she sees me. "Wow!" she says. "With your eye swollen shut like that, you look even worse than you did yesterday."

"Thanks. That's just what I needed to hear this morning," I tell her as we set off for school.

"Sorry. Does it hurt as much as it looks like it does?"

"No. Mostly it's just my lip that hurts. I'll have to try talking without moving my mouth."

"You know, Fritz, this is going to make a new person out of you. You're going to change from the kid with the knapsack to the kid who got beat up."

"If you're trying to make me feel better, it isn't working, Kath."

She looks embarrassed, but instead of apologizing, she says, "You know what? Either Lonny and Red are absent, or they're making a point of staying out of sight, 'cause I don't see them anywhere. They didn't come back to school yesterday, either, by the way."

I hear the bell, and since the two of them aren't running toward the building to shove their way inside, I figure they're absent. Boy, people will take one look at me and wonder what *they* must look like.

My beat-up face attracts a lot of attention at first, but as the day goes on the kids get used to seeing my bruises. Things sort of settle down. We're in the middle of English class when I hear a rumbling noise so loud it rattles the classroom windows. At first I don't think much about it, since we've heard rumblings coming from the canyons before, but this time it doesn't gradually die away. This time, it builds to a roar—a heavy, rolling sound that's worse than the loudest thunder I've ever heard.

I grab the sides of my desk and hang on for dear life, waiting for it to stop. Wondering if it ever will.

Wondering if the floor really is vibrating or if I'm imagining it. Nobody says a word—or if they do, I can't hear them—and nobody moves. It's like time's standing still. Finally, the thundering stops getting louder, and then it slowly begins to fade until it sounds far away rather than right here in the classroom.

When the last echo is gone I say, "The one you hear is never the one that gets you." There's some foot shuffling and throat clearing, but nobody says anything. I guess either the kids want to forget it happened, or else I've come too close to talking about what's going on in the Tech Area.

Since it's no use wishing I'd kept my mouth shut, I start wondering what was going on. Maybe the scientists were testing that "Gadget" they're always talking about, or maybe they were "tickling the dragon's tail." I've decided that *Gadget* has got to be the code name for whatever it is they're working on, and I figure *tickling the dragon's tail* must stand for some kind of really dangerous experiment.

Mrs. Evans picks up a couple of books that were knocked off her desk and the picture of President Roosevelt that was jarred off the wall, but her hands are shaking so much she has trouble getting the picture wire over the hook. Manny gets up to help her, and after she thanks him, she takes a deep breath and says, "Now, where were we, class?"

We all look at her blankly, and a strange expression crosses her face. She hesitates a moment, and I get the feeling she can't remember either. Finally, she says, "I'm going to let you use this time to work on those compositions that are due tomorrow." Nobody complains, which really shows how shaken we all are.

Since I finished my composition when I was home yesterday, I fish around in my knapsack and find Notes on the Secret Project. I open it to the section on Rumors and Observation, and shielding the page with my arm, I write: "Explosion shakes school building. Windows rattle. Books fall from edge of desk, picture shaken from wall." As I put the date beside my entry, I wish I'd checked the clock so I could say how long the rumbling lasted.

Class is almost over, so I start packing up my stuff. Everybody else is still working—or drawing, in some cases. Everybody but Kathy, that is, and she's just sitting there. She's got that same look she always has when she's thinking about her brother fighting over in Italy.

I don't want Kath to start in on how worried she is about Matthew, so I figure I'd better sidetrack her. "Since your dad's in ordnance, do you think he had something to do with that explosion?" I ask as we leave the building.

Kathy doesn't answer, and when I glance over at her I see that she's trying not to cry. "Hey, what's wrong?"

"What if it was an accident, and my dad was hurt? Or maybe killed?" Kathy's eyes are full of tears.

Great. Me and my big mouth. "You don't hear any sirens, do you? If it was an accident, we'd hear lots of sirens." Wouldn't we?

"You really think so?" Kathy asks, wiping her eyes.

Before I can answer, we hear another rumbling from one of the canyons. "Hear that?" I say triumphantly. "If they'd had an accident, they wouldn't be

81

doing more explosions."

"I guess you're right," Kathy says, fishing in her pocket for another tissue.

Boy, you sure do have to be careful what you say around here—and not just because of Security, either.

Chapter Twelve

"You're up early for a Saturday," Mom says when I come into the kitchen.

"Manny's going to show me some more ancient Indian stuff," I say, watching while she adds two more eggs to the skillet. "Do we have any waxed paper for me to wrap a couple of sandwiches in?"

She points to a cupboard and says, "Up there. Your face looks a lot less swollen today, incidentally."

"It feels a lot better, too," I tell her. Besides my sandwiches, I pack two small apples, figuring they might help me get in good with my horse.

When I get to the stable, Manny looks up from saddling Coal Dust and says, "You got some lunch in that knapsack of yours?"

"Yup. And a couple of apples to help me make friends with the horse."

"You don't have to worry about Brownie. She's so gentle my baby sister could ride on her."

I look at the mare Manny's saddled up for me, relieved to see that she's not nearly as big as Coal Dust. "Here, Brownie—want an apple?" I hold it on my palm like you're supposed to, steeling myself not to pull back my hand when she moves toward it. Her lips brush my fingers as she takes the fruit, and it feels like touching cool velvet. Like I imagine cool velvet would feel, anyhow.

"That wasn't so bad, now, was it?" Manny asks, grinning. I'll bet he really likes having the tables turned like this, with him being the expert and me being the one who doesn't know what the heck to do.

At least I've watched enough cowboy movies to know how to get on a horse, so I manage that all right. We go out of the corral, and as we head across the meadow, I hang on and don't look down, wondering how my sister can think this sort of thing is fun.

Pretty soon, Manny looks over his shoulder and asks, "You doin' okay?" When I nod, he says, "Good. Now we'll gallop."

"And on Monday I'll teach you calculus."

Manny laughs, so I figure I must have said the right thing. Feeling a bit more relaxed by now, I breathe in the crisp air and watch a flock of little birds swirl by. "What kind of birds are those, Manny?" I ask.

"Song sparrows," he says, "and that one over there is a snowbird." He gestures to a small, dark gray bird clinging to the seed head of a dried plant. I'm kind of disappointed, 'cause we have song sparrows and snowbirds at home. But I'll still write them down in my Flora and Fauna notebook when we stop.

Manny looks back at me again and says, "See the wall of the canyon way over there? It's got Indian rock art on it. You interested?"

"I sure am!"

"Come on, then. We'll ride cross country."

He picks up the pace, so it's a pretty bouncy ride. I wonder if we're trotting or cantering or what. We finally get over to where the canyon wall rises like the face of a cliff, and I say, "So where are all the petroglyphs?"

"The *what?*"

"The rock art."

Manny looks puzzled. "How come you called it petro-something?"

"Petroglyphs. My library book on ancient Indians calls it that."

"I'll bet your library book didn't tell you where to find yourself some petroglyphs," Manny says. "You need me for that. See where the rock is a darker brown?"

I look where he points, and there they are—"stylized symbols scratched into the rock"—exactly like the book said. Deer. Suns. Men dancing. While the horses graze and Manny eats his sandwiches, I fish in my knapsack for a pencil and get out Notes on Ancient Indians so I can copy the petroglyphs. Then I switch to Notes on Flora and Fauna and write down the names of those birds we saw.

After I eat my lunch, Manny says, "We'd better go on back, or tomorrow you'll be so sore you can't sit down."

"We have another composition to write for English class, too."

"I don't write no compositions," Manny says, standing up.

He's got this scornful look on his face, and it kind of rubs me the wrong way. "How the heck are you going to pass English if you don't do the assignments?"

"What am I gonna write about? I don't have no notebooks full of ideas like some people do."

"Your whole head is full of ideas," I tell him. "Didn't you say you've lived here all your life? And your ancestors before you?" He nods, and I see a hint of interest in his eyes. "Write about what this place was like before the army set up the Lab. Compare that to what it's like now. There's your composition."

The light in his eyes fades, and he says, "I have the idea for it maybe, but it ain't wrote down. And don't tell me to just write it down, 'cause you know I can't spell worth a darn."

"Yeah. You spell about as well as I ride." When he grins, I add, "Notice that I'm riding anyway."

"What you're doing ain't exactly riding, Fritz. Let's just say you're sitting on top of a horse."

And here I thought I was doing okay. He can go ahead and flunk English, if that's the way he's going to be.

Manny's leaning against the flagpole in the school yard with an I-hate-Mondays look on his face, and when he sees Kathy and me, he heads right toward us. Kath says, "Here comes your math student. See you later."

"Take a look at this," Manny says, thrusting a grubby-looking paper in my direction. It's creased and wrinkled like he's been carrying it around in his back pocket, and I wonder what the heck it is until I see "The Mesa" centered on the top line.

"This is your composition?"

Manny nods. "Tell me what you think of it."

I read it and figure it might get him a passing grade if it weren't so messy. And if more of the words were spelled right. And if it had some punctuation. "Let's just say you're sitting on top of a horse," I say as I hand back the paper.

His face falls. "That bad, huh?"

"Listen, Manny, we don't have English till the end of the day. You have lunch hour and a study period—plenty of time to copy that over and make some corrections."

He scowls and asks suspiciously, "What kind of corrections?"

"Capital letters and periods, for starts."

"If I'd of known where them things went, don't you think I'd of put 'em in?"

He starts to walk off, but I call to him, and when he stops, I say, "Read it out loud and put a period when your voice goes down. Start the next word with a capital."

A hopeful expression flits across his face. "That's all there is to it?"

"It's a start."

"I'll think about it," he says.

I hurry through lunch 'cause I want to get back to school in time to find something to read for my next book report. The minute I step outside, the cold settles in around me. It's a good thing I remembered to tell Kathy I was going back early so she won't be standing out here waiting for me.

I'm so sure I'll have the library to myself that I'm almost startled when I see Jacob reading at one of the tables.

"I didn't expect to find anybody else in here," I say when he looks up.

Jacob says, "This place is more welcoming than the schoolyard. Books do not draw away from me."

"And books don't try to beat me up. I never had a

chance to thank you for rescuing me that day, Jacob." Which is why people "draw away" from him. I wonder if he knows the kids call him the Human Tornado.

"I do not need thanks. It was something I had to do."

Jacob's eyes are starting to get a hard glint to them, so I quickly ask him what he's reading. Now he looks embarrassed. He shows me a copy of *American Boy* and says, "I improve my skill in reading English while perhaps I also learn not to be so different."

"Heck, I've been reading that magazine for a couple of years now, and I'm still different. But my dad says it's better to march to your own drummer than try to march to somebody else's and always be out of step."

Jacob frowns, and I figure he's trying to puzzle that out. "Your father means it is better to be your-self?" he asks. I nod, and he says, "You are fortunate to live in a place where that is allowed." His voice is flat now, and he turns his attention back to the magazine.

Remembering what I came in here for, I browse along the shelves until I find a biography of Thomas Edison. Then I sit down at the other end of the table from Jacob so he won't think I'm "drawing away" from him, and we both read until one o'clock.

The next afternoon I dash into my last period class two minutes late. Mrs. Evans frowns at me as she takes a paper from the folder on her desk, and I mutter, "Sorry." She gives an exaggerated sigh and looks down at the paper she's holding.

"Before I return the compositions you handed in yesterday, I'd like to read one of them aloud," she announces.

She's about to start when this new girl in the front row speaks up for the first time since she came here a couple of days ago. "Somebody *typed* their composition?" When I take a good look at her, I notice that she's pretty, in a delicate sort of way—pale, with blue eyes and light brown hair that turns under in a pageboy cut like my sister's.

"No, Gail," Mrs. Evans says, "I typed this myself, because the original paper was badly punctuated and difficult to read. I wanted to be able to do it justice, since once you get past all the errors, it's a good piece of writing."

"You mean it's good writing except for the writing?" I ask, pretty sure whose paper she's talking about.

Frowning again, Mrs. Evans says, "I mean that the content is quite good even though the English skills are poor." She clears her throat and begins. "The title is The Mesa. 'Before mankind came, the mesa rose from the desert floor. The air was fresh and smelled of the pine trees. In winter, the snow was white and marked by footprints of birds and animals. Then the Indians came. They brought the smell of wood smoke from their campfires and left the prints of their moccasins in the white snow. Then the Spanish came and planted their fields. The hoofprints of their horses were in the white snow.'"

Mrs. Evans clears her throat again. "'Much later, a man came and built a school for rich men's sons, but they respected the land. Then the army came with machines that chewed up the mesa and cut the pines and cottonwoods to make room for ugly green buildings. Now the air smells of exhaust. Now the snow is gray with dust from burning coal. Now the mesa is not proud. In less than two years, a place that stood proudly for a longer time than I can imagine has been spoiled, and I do not understand why.'"

For a moment, the classroom is silent, and then Kathy says, "I think it's a good composition, but I also think that dirty snow and smelly air and a few trees is a small price to pay if whatever they're doing at the Lab is going to end the war."

"That's true," I say, "but don't you think it's sort of interesting that even though we aren't being bombed by our enemies, part of our country is being destroyed because of the war?"

"A pretty small part, Fritz," Kathy says, her voice scornful. "And besides—"

"I'm going to have to stop this discussion," Mrs. Evans says, interrupting, "but I'd like to point out two things, class. The first is that good writing makes people think and ask questions, the way Kathy and Fritz were just now. And the second is the importance of choosing a topic you care about, as this student did."

"So who wrote it?" Kathy asks.

"Manny."

A couple of the kids congratulate him, and he slides a little lower in his chair.

Kathy raises her hand and asks if she can read her composition, and I figure it's that competitive streak of hers coming out—she probably wants to show off how much better her writing is than Manny's. But when she gets up in front of the class, she isn't wearing that I-thought-you-said-you-were-good-at-ping-pong look of hers. She just seems sort of eager. Enthusiastic.

"The title of my composition is 'The German

Madam Curie,'" she announces, and then she begins to read. At first I listen because I want to find out whether Kathy's as good at writing as she is in math—which she is. Pretty soon, though, I'm listening because I want to know more about this woman scientist's life. Because I want to know how she got out of Germany.

When Kathy finishes reading, Manny says, "If you got some of your information from an interview, that must mean this Lise Meitner you wrote about works over at the Lab, right?"

Kathy shakes her head. "She's in Sweden. I interviewed somebody from the Lab who knew her in Europe. Somebody who was inspired by her."

Helga. That's who she interviewed. How come Kathy never mentioned anything about that? Hey, I wonder if she found out anything we can put in Notes on the Secret Project. I doubt it. Helga's probably too smart to let anything slip. After all, Kathy's composition was about the woman's *life*, not about her work.

At the end of class, Mrs. Evans asks Manny to stay behind, and I wait for him in the hall, since we'll be going to the library for our after-school math session. Kathy waits, too, and I'm glad to see she's not mad because I disagreed with her in class.

"Great composition, Kath," I tell her.

"Thanks. I used to want to be a writer, but now I think maybe I'll be some kind of scientist, instead."

I'm about to say maybe she could write about science when Manny comes out of the classroom. Right away, Kathy pounces on him and asks, "So what did she want?"

"Aw, she says I gotta stay late twice a week to

91

work on my writing skills. You don't do your homework, she makes you stay late. You *do* your homework, and you still have to stay." He turns to me and says, "I tried to tell her you was helping me with my math, but she just said, 'No excuses. I'll see you Tuesdays and Thursdays.'"

I glance around to make sure Lonny and Red didn't hear Manny say that. I figure as long as they think I'm staying late every day to work with him, they won't be waiting for me after school.

Manny heads for the library with his math homework, but before I follow him I turn to Kathy and ask, "Have you had a chance to find out anything about that new girl's father?"

"I asked her, but she said she didn't think she was supposed to talk about it. She did invite me to come over after school tomorrow, though. Her family's living in one of the prefabs until their apartment is ready. Wouldn't it be great if Gail moved into the apartment building that's going up back of where I live?"

"Yeah," I agree as I open the library door. Kathy needs a girl friend the same as I need friends who are guys. Like Manny—and maybe Jacob.

Chapter Thirteen

The morning sun on the snow is almost blinding. "Wow!" I exclaim, squinting out the window, "I didn't know they ever got this much snow around here. Those drifts look almost like sand dunes."

From the kitchen, Mom says, "Quite an improvement over all those layers of coal dust, isn't it?"

"Yeah. Covers up that army green, too. Listen—that sounds like somebody shoveling our steps."

"The U.S. Army, at your service, no doubt," Dad says, joining me at the window.

Good. That means I won't have to do it. Mom calls us to breakfast, and I do a double take at the sight of plates piled high with pancakes instead of the usual bowls of cereal.

"The commissary was out of milk again yesterday," Mom says as we take our places at the table. "That's twice this week. I certainly hope the army does a better job of supplying our troops overseas."

Dad stares glumly into his cup and says, "I can't drink my coffee black," but Mom downs hers like a medicine. I dig into my pancakes—which taste fine made without milk. I figure the commissary runs out of stuff because the army supplies the troops overseas before it sends groceries to army posts here at home. Still, I'm glad Kathy didn't hear Mom's crack, 'cause Kath doesn't need to start worrying about whether her brother has enough to eat. Whether he has enough ammunition. . . .

After breakfast I bundle up to go outside, figuring a day like this one shouldn't be wasted. Timmy, from downstairs, is already out there, making a row of snow angels. "Hi, Fritz," he calls. "Want to help?"

"How about you help me make a snowman, instead."

"Later."

Later I'll be in school. I scoop up a handful of snow, but it's too powdery to pack into a ball. I'm thinking that it would make for fast sledding when I see Kathy coming, huddled inside her coat. She has on a plaid muffler, and she's got it wrapped around so it covers her nose and mouth.

"Isn't this great, Kath?" I call.

"I guess it's great if you live in a nice, cozy apartment," she says, "but I keep thinking of Matthew trying to keep warm in even more snow than this. Living in some kind of tent."

The other day, she had him living in a foxhole, but I'm not going to argue about it. Neither of us says much on the way to school. She's worrying about her brother, and I'm wishing I hadn't waited for her—and feeling guilty for wishing it. After all, she listens when I'm worrying about Lonny and Red.

All morning my eyes keep straying to the classroom windows, only now I'm looking at the drifts in the school yard instead of the jagged mountains in the distance. Too bad it's warming up—the snow's already starting to melt.

It's finally noon, and everybody bundles up and starts home for lunch. I'm kind of enjoying the *fwumph, fwumph, fwumph* our galoshes make in the snow as we cross the schoolyard when a snowball sails past my left ear and another one hits my shoulder, hard. That powdery snow must have melted enough to pack, and I don't have to look around to know that Lonny and Red are the ones taking advantage of it.

Snowballs at forty paces is a lot more my style than fists at arm's length, so I crouch to scoop up a handful of snow. I'm squeezing it into shape when I see Lonny aiming his next one right at me. I duck to the side, then spring up and let loose with my snowball. Got 'im! The next one I throw has Red's name on it. Just missed. Ha! That one didn't. We'll have to change his name to Snow White.

I see that Kathy's made a bunch of snowballs, and I start to take one from the pile, but she yells, "Hey, keep your hands off those!"

"Sorry," I say as I pack my next handful of snow. "I thought you were making them for me." She lets one fly, and it hits Lonny square in the chest. Mine misses. Now I see Kathy's strategy. She's bombarding those guys with one snowball after another, and they can't seem to decide whether to dodge them or make more snowballs of their own.

Lonny suddenly wheels around, and the back of his jacket has a big splat of snow on it. *Manny!* And Jacob's running up to join him. Lonny and Red are caught in the crossfire now, and they don't know who to throw at first.

I decide to try Kathy's strategy, and pretty soon we've got some real teamwork going. I make a bunch of ammunition while she throws hers, and then I throw mine while she makes a new supply. Meanwhile, Jacob has become a human throwing machine—make a snowball, throw it, make another, throw it. Manny's slower, but more of his shots find their target.

I hardly notice the snowballs that are hitting my body, but I'm stunned for a moment when a really hard-packed one slams me in the chest. Holy cow! That felt like a rock!

Lonny's cheer is cut short by one of Jacob's fast shots that hits him on the back of his head and then sort of slides down inside his coat collar. He looks like he's doing some kind of dance, trying to get it out. Red looks over to see what's going on, and Manny lets loose with one that whops him upside the head.

Kathy just threw the last one on her pile, so I start in with mine. They all have Lonny's name on 'em, and I let them fly, one after the other: Miss. Miss. Hit. Miss. Hit. And all the time, the Throwing Machine is methodically alternating between Lonny and Red, always aiming for the backs of their heads or their faces so some of the snow goes down their necks.

Finally someone yells, "Halt!" and everybody freezes in place. I look around, but there's nobody here but the six of us. The same voice calls, "I declare a cease-fire until further notice. Abandon your weapons and return to your quarters."

Holy cow! That was *Jacob.* We all stand there staring at him for a moment, and then Red looks at Lonny, like he's waiting for a cue, and without a word, Lonny stalks away. The rest of us watch them go, and then Jacob pulls off a mitten and raises his hand in the V for Victory sign. Silently, the rest of us do the same, and then we all head for home.

"That was fun!" Kathy says. Her cheeks are red and her eyes sparkle, and without her usual discontented expression she's actually pretty.

"We really let 'em have it, Kath. I guess four-against-two wasn't exactly fair, but I sure enjoyed seeing them get the worst of it."

Kathy says, "Two-against-one wasn't exactly fair when they beat you up that day, either. They got what was coming to them."

"Guess I don't have to ask who taught you to throw like that." Too bad I couldn't have had a big brother like Matthew instead of an older sister.

I'm buttoning my heavy jacket, thinking what luck it is that this new snow fell on the weekend instead of a school day, when I notice that Dad isn't getting ready. "Hey, aren't you going to the ski slope with us?" I ask.

It seems a long time before he says, "Not this time, Fritz."

Something in his voice warns me not to ask why, so I follow Mom outside. Blinking in the brilliant sunlight, we clomp down the stairs, skis on our shoulders, and walk toward the road to catch the army bus that goes to Sawyer's Hill. The air is so cold it feels like I'm inhaling tiny knives, but I manage to ask, "How come Dad's staying home?"

Mom sighs. "He's been feeling a bit low lately, Fritz."

"You mean run down from always working late?"

"Low spirited," Mom says. "It would do him a world of good to get some fresh air and exercise, but you can't tell him anything."

Uh-oh. "Are things going badly at the Lab?"

"My sense is that things are moving along well," Mom says. "Between you and me, I think your father's having second thoughts about being involved in the project."

Second thoughts about working to end the war? I puzzle about that till I see Kathy waving to us. The new girl, Gail, is with her, and I remember that on Friday, Kathy was all excited because Gail's family was moving into one of the just-finished apartment buildings.

The bus pulls up, and when everybody forms a line, I see that both girls have two parents with them. I sure wish Dad hadn't stayed home—especially since Sunday is the only time families can be together.

"Where's Verne?" Kathy's father asks as he stands up to give Mom the seat next to his wife.

"He didn't feel quite up to enjoying himself."

Kathy's mother says, "I think there's a lot of that going around. Almost an epidemic, wouldn't you say?"

Already I'm planning what I'm going to write under Rumors and Observations. Maybe "Scientists bend under heavy work load." Maybe "Scientists discouraged by—" By what? Not by lack of progress, I hope.

The driver calls, "If you're standing in the aisle, please move toward the rear of the bus. We still got a couple more stops to make."

I'm moving back when someone calls to me. Jacob! I make my way toward where he's sitting, hoping this means he wants to be friends. After he introduces me to his father, he says, "I did not know you are a skier."

"I'm a complete beginner. I've only skied once before, when our family spent Christmas with relatives in Pennsylvania. We get a lot of snow where I come from, but there aren't any mountains."

Jacob's father says, "Denmark also is a flat place, and the part of England where we lived as well. It is good to be again in a place with mountains."

The three of us chat a little more, then lapse into silence. I concentrate on keeping my footing as the crowded bus makes its way up the steep winding road. Finally the driver pulls over and calls, "End of the line, folks!"

We all scramble off the bus with our skis, and I introduce Jacob and his father to Mom. While the three of them are saying all the usual things, she sort of searches Jacob's face with her eyes, and I realize she's looking for signs of the Human Tornado. Today, though, he's just a polite kid going skiing with his father.

Since Mom already has her skis on, I tell her not to wait for me. I pretend to have trouble with my bindings, but really I'm listening to Jacob's father remind him to bend his knees, watching Jacob's father demonstrate how to shift his weight to change direction. I'm also hoping they'll ask me to join them, but they don't.

Dad should have come. . . .

The first thing I notice when we get home from skiing is the smell of stale cigarette smoke. Mom picks up the overflowing ashtray from the table by Dad's easy chair and says, "Your father must be taking a nap." Wrinkling her nose, she holds the ashtray at arm's length and goes to empty it into the garbage can on the balcony.

When she comes back inside, I ask, "When did

Dad start to smoke so much, anyhow?"

"I'm not sure. When things started to get really tense over at the Lab, I expect. This place does reek, doesn't it?"

"Things are tense at the Lab? Because the project isn't—um, working?"

Mom shrugs off her jacket and says, "Because they're facing a deadline. They're working so hard over there that your father scarcely has time to breathe."

"You mean the Germans are ahead of them?" But how could they be, after all the Allied bombings I've been reading about?

"That's not what I mean at all, Fritz, and you know very well I can't tell you anything more. At least you ought to know that by this time."

Mom disappears into the kitchen, and I stomp down the hall to my room, envying my sister who gets to live with Grandma. I don't exactly slam the door, but I shut it hard enough to make it obvious I'm not pleased with the way I'm treated around here. If I've disturbed Dad's nap, that's too bad.

I open the Secret Project notebook to my favorite section—Rumors and Observations—and read the whole thing, just to get my mind off my hurt feelings.

I feel a lot better by the time I finish. Mom doesn't have to tell me anything—I can find stuff out by myself. After today's date I write: "In spite of the fact that the project is going well and is ahead of the German efforts, many scientists are feeling tense because they are facing a deadline."

A deadline for what? Finishing the project?

Chapter Fourteen

I'm trudging home through a misty snow, carrying Dad's paper inside my coat to keep it dry, when Kathy catches up to me. "Where are you coming back from?" I ask her.

"The commissary." She holds up a small bag and says, "Mom forgot to buy whipping cream. You wouldn't believe how many ration points this was, but she wants to make eggnog to bring to your mother's Christmas Eve party."

"Between having all the neighbors over tonight and inviting a bunch of the unmarried scientists for Christmas dinner tomorrow, I think Mom's making sure she won't have time to miss my sister." Before Kathy can start in about missing Matthew, I quickly change the subject. "Isn't it great that we're having a white Christmas?"

"Without Matthew, it won't seem like Christmas, no matter how much snow we have."

So much for changing the subject. I'm trying to imagine tomorrow morning without Grandma and Vivian when I realize Kathy's saying something more.

"Back home, the whole holiday season used to be a really special time, but here on the Hill, we're lucky to get a holiday twenty-four hours. Sometimes it seems like people are just going through the motions because they feel obligated, but nobody's heart is really in it."

An army truck full of carolers passes us, and I say, "Sounds like their hearts are in it."

"They're probably just putting up a good front."

What a Scrooge. "Maybe you ought to try that for a change, Kathy. Afterall, you aren't the only person in this country who has a brother—or maybe a husband or father—overseas."

"*Okay*, Fritz. Look, I understand that it's wartime and that we're here for an important reason. I understand that Matthew has to fight to stop the Nazis and protect our freedom. But understanding doesn't make me like it any better."

We squinch along on the powdery snow, and now I'm feeling like a Scrooge for upsetting Kathy. And on Christmas Eve, too. The silence stretches out so long I start to feel nervous. Finally, I say, "So, is your building having a holiday feast tomorrow like you all did at Thanksgiving?"

"And like we did last Christmas and last Thanksgiving," Kathy says. "I'm getting so used to spending holidays with neighbors instead of relatives that it's starting to feel normal. Do you think we'll be back home by this time next year?"

She sounds so forlorn that I feel like kicking myself for getting mad at her. "Gosh, Kath, I don't know. We're definitely winning, but the war news hasn't been so good lately." I think of the fighting going on in Europe right now, with the Nazis trying to hold off the Allies as they fight their way closer to Germany. The Battle of the Bulge is what they're calling it. Even the name has a bad sound.

The silence starts to stretch out again, but this

time Kathy breaks it. "Matt always loved Christmas. It's his favorite holiday. I really, really hope he doesn't have to fight on Christmas Day."

Doesn't have to kill on Christmas Day—that's what she means. I wonder if Kathy reads the headlines, if she saw that one the other day, something about the Allied offensive in Italy being "stalled by stiff defenses." Sounds pretty bad.

That truckload of carolers drives past again. Their song floats across the dusk, and I catch a few words: *. . . of peace on earth, good will to men.*

Kathy and I look at each other, then look away. I guess we're both wondering if there will ever be a time when those words are true.

I finish the last of the books I got for Christmas, and I'm thinking about heading off to the library when somebody knocks.

"Guess what?" Kathy says the second I open the door. "I read in *The Daily Bulletin* that the skating rink's finally open—want to try out those ice skates you got for Christmas?"

"Sure. Where is this rink, anyway?"

"They flood the floor of one of the canyons," Kathy says, wiping her feet before she comes inside. "An army bus takes everybody down there—get your skates and let's go."

I bundle up, grab my shiny clip-on skates, and follow Kathy down the stairs. "Say, isn't there going to be snow all over the ice?"

"Don't worry about it," Kathy says, and when we get off the bus down at the rink, I see that the ice is clear. I also see wood stacked beside a bonfire.

"The U.S. Army at work?" I ask. She nods, and I remember what Mom said, something about how keeping the scientists' families happy is important for the war effort because it's a way of making sure the scientists aren't distracted from the project. Still, I can see how the soldiers would resent "babysitting a bunch of longhairs," like I heard some of them complaining about in the PX the other day.

We strap on our skates at the edge of the ice, and I'm relieved to see that Kathy's only an average skater, same as I am, 'cause if she was really good, she'd be skating circles around me. Literally.

I'm having a great time and doing okay, especially for the first time on the ice this winter, when somebody comes crashing into me. I hit the ice, skid a couple of yards on my shoulder and hip, and knock the feet out from under some WAC who lands on top of me.

By the time we're both standing up again and through apologizing, I have a pretty good idea who it was that bowled me over, 'cause if it had been an accident, somebody would have come over by now to say they were sorry.

I look around for Kathy and see her skating toward me. "Bad news," she says. "Lonny and Red are down here."

"Yeah, I just found that out the hard way. But we aren't going to let them run us off the ice. Come on, Kath, let's skate."

My shoulder hurts a lot, but it's not broken or anything, and soon I'm having a good time again. A bunch of kids on the far side of the rink are playing crack the whip, so I make a point of staying out of their way. Great. Looks like they're coming over here—and the whip-cracker is Lonny.

I try to skate out of the way, but the next thing I know, I'm airborne. And then I hit the ice. Hard.

The *next* thing I know, this big guy is carrying me off the ice. Somebody gets a log from the woodpile for him to set me down on, and there's a bunch of people standing there staring at me. At least nobody's yelling "Fight! Fight!"

After a couple of minutes I look around for Kathy. One of the upper school girls who's warming her hands at the fire says, "Your friend went to ask the bus driver if he'd wait till you could get over there."

"Thanks. Guess I'd better go, then."

The big guy says, "Need any help, sport?"

"Wouldn't mind if you skated alongside me." There's no way I'm going out on that ice by myself as long as Lonny's anywhere around.

Kathy's waiting for me, and I don't complain when she kneels down to unbuckle my skates and then carries them for me. I follow her to the bus and manage to haul myself on board. "So you're the kid who had the accident, are you?" the driver says. "You and your friend take that front seat I saved for you."

I sink down into it. My head feels big as a pumpkin, and I ache all over, but at least this time there's no blood. I lean back and close my eyes, and besides making me feel a little better, it keeps Kathy from talking to me. She doesn't say a word till she tells me our stop is coming up.

"You take care of yourself, now, kid," the driver says when we get off.

"No matter what you say, I'm coming home with

you," Kathy announces once we're outside.

I don't argue with her, and when we get into the apartment, she says, "You sit down on the sofa, and I'll bring you a glass of water."

After I drink about half of it, I say, "Listen, Kathy, if you tell your parents about my 'accident' down at the rink, leave Lonny's name out it, okay?"

"Okay, if that's what you want, but I don't see why."

"Because if what really happened ever gets back to my mom, she'll march right over to the school and have them pull Lonny out of class so she can read him the riot act. And I don't need that."

Kathy agrees, and as she starts to leave, I say, "There's one other thing, Kath—thanks."

"Friends look out for each other, Fritz," she says. "Hope you feel better soon."

I watch her leave, thinking that I'd have a hard time looking out for anybody else when I can't even look out for myself—and realizing that I still have a lot to learn about being friends.

"Lonny's telling everybody he really fixed you down at the skating rink on Saturday," Manny says when we meet in the library for our math session on the first day back from Christmas vacation.

I open my eyes wider and say, "He's *what?* Lonny wasn't even down at the rink on Saturday. At least, if he was, I didn't see him." Boy, am I ever glad Kathy tipped me off that Lonny was bragging about what he'd done to me.

Manny gives me a long look and says, "Are you telling me you wasn't practically knocked out by them boys playing crack-the-whip?"

"That part's true, all right, but Lonny didn't have anything to do with it. I got in the way, that's all. He must have heard what happened and decided to take the credit to make himself look good, or something. He's bound to have heard about it, 'cause lots of kids from school were there."

"Well, if he ain't something. Just wait till I tell the guys about that. Nobody's gonna believe a word he says after this."

Apparently I'm not such a bad liar after all—as long as I can plan out what I'm going to say ahead of time. I open my math book, and Manny takes out the quiz paper he got back today so we can go over his mistakes. Mostly just careless ones this time. I feel a little guilty about lying to him, but they say that all's fair in love and war, and this business with Lonny is as close as I ever want to come to being personally involved in a war.

I'm still feeling good about turning the tables on Lonny when I set out for the PX. I'm standing there, reading the headlines while I wait to pay for the paper, when I hear a mocking voice.

"Hey, Fritzy-Witzy. How'd you like being carried off the ice down at the rink Saturday?"

I count out my coins, then turn to face Lonny. "Not much. But it was my own fault—I got in the way of some kids playing crack-the-whip. Next time I'll have to be more careful."

The self-satisfied look on Lonny's face changes to disbelief, and I walk out of the PX feeling great. Except for my shoulder, and it feels a lot better than it did on Saturday.

Chapter Fifteen

Just about everybody—including the teacher—has one of those sour Monday morning faces on, so I'm kind of surprised at how cheerful Kathy looks when she and Gail dash into the classroom. A lot more cheerful than Saturday afternoon, that's for sure.

I spend most of science class thinking about what a great time we had skiing and how I finally managed to get down that long trail through the woods without falling once. It was a perfect day till we were on the army bus coming back from Sawyer's Hill. That's when I made the mistake of saying something about how easy it was to forget the war once we got away from town and all the soldiers and MPs and the army-green buildings. All of a sudden, Kath started feeling guilty about how she'd been *enjoying* the snow while Matthew was trying to *survive* in it. And then she told us how long it had been since they'd had a letter and how worried she was about him. Boy, it's a good thing Gail was there, 'cause I never know what to do when somebody looks like they might start crying any minute.

Finally class is over, and Kathy bounces up to me and announces, "Matthew's fine. We got a whole batch of letters in Saturday's mail."

"That's great, Kath. I'm really glad." I guess Kathy

doesn't realize she only knows that Matthew was fine when he wrote the last of those letters. Something could have happened to him since then. Something like getting shot. Gail's waiting for Kathy, and when our eyes meet, I'm pretty sure she's thinking the same thing I am.

Fourth period is social studies, which used to be my favorite subject till Mrs. Jackson started having current events discussions. I'm hoping this is going to be one of the days we actually learn something when she zeroes in on me and says, "Fritz, what do you think is the most significant thing in the news the last day or two?"

"Probably the Russians liberating that concentration camp in Poland," I tell her.

"Could you tell us why you find that significant, Fritz?"

Before I have a chance to answer, Gail says, "I can't believe that anybody could treat other human beings the way those people were treated. Those pictures—"

I stop listening. That's why I hate these discussions. Instead of *thinking* about what's happened and trying to figure out what it all means, everybody wants to *talk* about it. Well, let 'em talk. I'll enjoy the view.

The snow-covered mountains stand out against the sky, and I decide that next time we're assigned a composition for English, I'll compare the Jemez Mountains in winter to the volcano that used to be here. I'll use lots of phrases like "boldly white against an azure sky" for the mountains and words like "fiery" for the volcano. Mrs. Evans gives extra credit if we use words from our vocabulary lessons.

I glance at the clock. Only a couple more minutes of this, thank goodness. Suddenly, I hear somebody running down the hall—a boy, from the sound of it—and I wince when the outside door to the building crashes open. Whoever it was didn't even slow down, just hit that metal piece that goes across the door and barreled on through.

"Stay in your seats, class," Mrs. Jackson says, and she sounds so stern—especially for her—that we all do. Clicking footsteps in the hall now, somebody in a hurry but not quite running. A teacher, but she's way too late to stop him. *To stop Jacob.* That was the sound of leather shoes, not boots. Not sneakers.

I hear kids' voices in the hall now, and Manny says, "Can't you let us out early this one time? We ain't gonna learn nothin' in the next two minutes."

There's a chorus of voices saying "Yeah," and "Come on, Mrs. Jackson," and while she's trying to decide, I slip on my knapsack, just in case.

"All right, class. You're dismissed," she says, and I'm the first one out of the classroom.

As soon as I catch the words *Human Tornado,* I ask one of the girls standing in a group by the door, "Did he hit anybody?"

She shakes her head. "And nobody did a thing to him, either. I was right smack in the middle of reading my composition to the class when he ran out."

"What was your composition about?" I ask her.

"We were supposed to take a news article and rewrite it in first person. You know, using *I* or *we* instead of *he* or *they?*" I nod, and the girl says, "Anyhow, I picked an article about how Allied troops freed

110

the Jews who'd been locked up in that concentration camp, and I wrote it like I was one of the soldiers describing what I saw."

"It was a really good composition," adds one of the other girls. "Too bad we didn't get to hear the rest of it."

Jacob didn't want to hear the rest of it, so he ran. I remember the newspaper headlines and those photos I didn't want to look at. Was Jacob thinking that his family could have ended up in a camp like that—or was he thinking about friends and relatives who did?

Mrs. Evans is standing in the doorway of our classroom, talking to Mrs. Jackson, and even though I edge closer, I can only hear part of what she's saying. ". . . react like that . . . without his coat in this cold . . . psychologist . . . ."

A heavy feeling settles in my chest as I realize Jacob has just given the kids another reason to draw away from him. As if they needed one.

Chapter Sixteen

When I come into the library, I see Jacob at a table by himself and the rest of the kids from his class sitting on the other side of the room, as far away from him as they can get. It's been a couple days now since he dashed out of class and ran home, but this is the first time I've seen him since then.

I sit down opposite him and open my three-hole binder, making it obvious that I'm going to be working here. Jacob glances up, and I see these dark shadows under his eyes, like he's been up all night or something. He looks relieved to see that it's me—or rather, *I*, since his grammar is always perfect.

"Be right back," I whisper, and I go to look for that book with the chapter on the volcanic history of this area so I can take some notes for my English composition. I find the reference book and take my place across from Jacob. The more I read, the more it strikes me that it would be more accurate to call him the Human *Volcano*—the pressure building up below the surface and then the violent explosion as it bursts out.

A couple of minutes before the period ends, everybody else starts gathering up their things, but since Manny's going to be coming in to work on math in a couple of minutes, I keep on reading. Jacob leaves without saying goodbye, and I try not to mind.

Pretty soon, Manny whomps his books on the table and sits down at right angles to me. "So what are you doin' your composition on that you've gotta do *re*search?" he asks.

"On the Jemez Mountains," I tell him, closing the book.

"The *what* mountains?"

I tell him again, and he says, "How do you spell them 'Zhemmay' Mountains?

"J-E-M-E-Z."

"That's pronounced 'Haymez,' Fritz. It's Spanish. Don't you remember Miz Jackson talkin' about them when we did geography last fall?"

I can feel my face getting red. "Yeah, and I never could find them on the map."

"Then how come you could get a hundred percent on your geography test, like you did?"

"It was a written test, Manny. It didn't ask me to locate the H-A-Y-M-E-Z Mountains, it asked me to locate the J-E-M-E-Z Mountains, and I could find those 'Zhemmay' Mountains without any trouble." I ham it up a little, to sort of give Manny permission to laugh.

And he does. He throws back his head and laughs. And laughs. I start to laugh, too, and pretty soon we both have tears running down our cheeks.

Mrs. Evans comes in and says, "What on earth is going on? I can hear you two all the way down the hall."

I wipe my eyes on my sleeve and say, "Manny's helping me with that composition you assigned. I'm writing it on the Zhemmay Mountains."

"On *what?*"

That's all it takes to set us off again. Mrs. Evans looks baffled, and I manage to pull myself together enough to explain. "Ah," she says. "I wondered what kind of help Manny was giving you." She frowns, as if that didn't come out quite the way she meant it to, and then she leaves.

The minute the library door closes behind her, Manny and I explode with laughter again. "Did you hear that? She wondered what kind of help you were giving me!"

The next thing we know, Mrs. James is standing beside us, her hands on her hips. She's a tall, straight-up-and-down kind of woman, and because of the way she wears her hair pulled back in a bun, she always looks sort of stern. Now, though, she looks down-right grim.

"Is this the way you help Manny with his math, Fritz?"

I get serious real fast. "No, ma'am."

"This is how I help Fritz, here, with his English composition, Miz James," Manny tells her.

I can't help myself. I try to hold it back, but a huge snort of a laugh bursts out of me.

Mrs. James draws herself up even taller, and she's opening her mouth to say something when Mrs. Evans opens the door and beckons to her. "I need to see you right away," she says.

"I'll be there as soon as I—"

"*Now*, Irma," Mrs. Evans says in the same tone of voice she sometimes uses in class, and Mrs. James stalks out of the library without another word.

Manny and I dissolve on the spot. Every time one of us starts to get under control, the other one says, "'*Now*, Irma.'"

Finally, I wipe my eyes again and start to pack my

knapsack, and Manny picks up his books. Guess we both know we wouldn't get much work done today.

We're heading for the door when I hear laughter coming from the social studies room and then Mrs. Jackson's voice saying, "*Zhemmay* Mountains? Fritz actually thought that's what they were called?"

Manny elbows me and says, "Could be worse, Fritz. Could be the kids laughin' at you instead of just the teachers."

"I know one thing," I tell him, "Mrs. Evans won't dare read my composition aloud in class." And I know something else, too—Manny and I are friends. I was pretty sure we were, but now I'm positive.

I'm looking out the living room window, thinking about how everybody talks about "the mountains," not "the *Jemez* Mountains," when Mom calls us to breakfast. The whole time I'm spooning up my cream of wheat I'm wondering how I'm going to look any of my teachers in the eye today. Or anytime soon.

Once I get to school, it doesn't take me long to figure out that the teachers don't want to look me in the eye either. Probably afraid they'll start laughing. The good thing about it is that I don't get called on when I don't have my hand up, which means I won't get called on during the social studies discussion.

Today Mrs. Jackson asks Manny to tell her what he thinks is the most significant news article of the past few days. Since that's how she always starts these discussions, everybody's caught on to preparing an answer for that question, just in case.

"The firebombing of Berlin and Dresden, over in Germany," Manny says confidently.

"And why do you think this is significant?"

That's always her next question, and Manny's prepared for it, too. "'Cause more than a thousand planes dropped a whole lot of tons of bombs over there, and some of the bombs caused fires that used up all the oxygen and sucked up everything from miles around. A firestorm, they called it. The whole city was destroyed."

"Serves 'em right," Red calls out. "Them Krauts deserve to be burned up. Burned alive," he adds.

Gail raises her hand and asks, "Mrs. Jackson, do you think maybe next time you could ask for the most significant article that isn't about battles or concentration camps or destroying cities and burning people alive?"

"That sounds like a really good idea," Kathy says, trying to make herself heard above the *boos* coming from the back row where Lonny and Red sit. "Can we try it, Mrs. Jackson?" she asks.

Mrs. Jackson hesitates, and Gail says, "Maybe we could vote."

Mrs. Jackson asks for a show of hands, and it's a tie, split with all the girls in favor of the change, and all the boys against it except for this German kid named Dietrich.

"We ought to vote again, 'cause *somebody* ain't voting," Red says, and I can feel his eyes burning into the back of my neck.

Kathy turns around in her seat and says scornfully, "You can't keep on voting till it turns out the way you want, you know."

I turn around, too, and Red's still glaring at me. "Sometimes people abstain," I tell him. "You don't have to vote on something if you don't care which way it turns out." And I don't care what the class talks about, 'cause I'm not planning to listen.

We end up spending the whole period talking about voting and secret ballots and politics and all kinds of interesting stuff, and when I'm on my way out of the room, Mrs. Jackson says, "You made some very thoughtful contributions to our discussion today, Fritz."

Good grief. I never even realized that was a discussion. I'm glancing up and down the hallway, keeping an eye out for Lonny and Red, when I see they've got Dietrich pinned to the wall. Probably taunting him about voting with the girls, but better him than me— I figured they'd have it in for me 'cause I refused to vote at all, and I can't help feeling relieved that they're picking on Dietrich, instead. As I go by, he flashes me this pleading look, but I pretend not to notice and keep right on walking. The last thing I need is to have those goons start in on me again.

I'm almost to the door when I hear a commotion. When I turn around to see what's going on, I see Kathy and Gail reading the goons the riot act. I can't hear what the girls are saying, but I catch the phrase "acting like Nazis." While Lonny and Red are distracted, Dietrich slips away from them. I hold the door open for him, and as he goes past, he gives me this look. A look that says, *Thanks a lot, you coward.*

Great. I head on home for lunch without waiting for the girls. . . .

At the beginning of English period, I ask permission to work on my composition in the library again, and Mrs. Evans agrees. I take my place opposite

Jacob, but he doesn't look up. His books are closed, and he's writing something—he's filled nearly half a page already. Except for a pair of girls by the window, the two of us are the only ones in here today.

By the time I've taken some notes on the "Haymez" Mountains, Jacob is almost to the bottom of his paper. I frown when I notice that the precise European handwriting at the beginning of the page has become almost a scrawl.

Suddenly, he pushes back his chair, and in a few long strides he's out of the library. I make it to the hall in time to see the outside door close behind him. I walk slowly back to the table and sit staring across it at Jacob's paper, wishing I could read upside down. Somehow, that wouldn't seem as wrong as picking it up and reading it—which is what I really want to do. Which is what I'm going to do.

The two girls who were working over by the windows walk past on their way out, and as soon as the door shuts behind them, I reach across the table for Jacob's paper. When I see the title, I get a dull feeling in the pit of my stomach.

Dresden
My parents grew up in Dresden, and although I have never been to that city, all my life I have heard of its glories. My mother has told me of the museums and galleries filled with priceless art. My father has told me of the magnificent architecture.

Now the handwriting is harder to read. More cramped. I bend closer to the paper, trying to decipher the words.

Perhaps I would never see this city where gen-erations of my family had lived, but I knew that it was there.

It was there until February 14, 1945, when the bombs rained down and the fires raged and more bombs and more fires and everything was destroyed and still more bombs and

And that's when he couldn't stand any more, when he—left. My heart is pounding as I stare at those last, almost illegible lines, and I give a start when the library door opens and Mrs. Jackson comes in.

"Hi, Fritz," she says. "Have you seen Jacob? He asked if he could come here to write an essay instead of taking part in the current events discussion."

"Um, he left. This is his essay."

I hand it to her, and she begins to read. "The poor boy," she whispers. "No wonder he runs off."

Gesturing at the paper, I say, "I guess I shouldn't have read it."

Mrs. Jackson looks at me and blinks, like she'd forgotten I was here, and then she says, "Maybe he wanted you to read it. He could have taken his paper with him, you know."

Wanted me to read it? But *why?* So I'd know things he couldn't talk about, maybe. I'm still puzzling over this when I hear a commotion in the hall and realize school's over for the day and Mrs. Jackson's on her way out of the library with Jacob's things. I close my reference book as Manny comes in. He whomps down his stuff, I get my math book out of my knapsack, and we start to work.

Chapter Seventeen

"Hey, where's Dad?" I ask when I see the break-fast table set for two.

Mom finishes pouring our juice before she says, "All I know is that he's going to be away for a few days and that it has something to do with his work."

That may be all she *knows,* I think as I take my place at the table, but I'll bet she could make a pretty good guess. You can't tell me she doesn't hear things over at the Tech Area. Heck, for all I know, she types up all kinds of secret stuff for her boss, whoever he is.

Before I can stop myself, I ask, "How come you still won't tell me who you work for over at the Lab?"

"Because sometimes you're too curious for your own good, Fritz, and you don't always think before you speak."

Like right now.

"Remember, Fritz, those 'Loose Lips Sink Ships' posters aren't just for decoration."

Boy, she sure is in a bad mood. I excuse myself and take my dishes to the sink, hoping the rest of the day goes better than the first hour has. I'm check-ing over the composition I wrote last night when Mom comes to my room to say she's leaving for work. "See you later," I tell her.

She's been gone about a minute when somebody bangs on the door. I open it, and Kathy bursts in.

"Quick," she says. "Get your Secret Project notebook and open it to Rumors and Observations." I dash to my room to grab my knapsack, and she calls after me, "Bring a pencil." As if I wouldn't.

By the time I'm back, she's taken off her coat and is sitting at the kitchen table like she belongs there. "What's this all about?" I ask her, slipping into my usual seat.

She leans forward and says, "Last night I had a babysitting job up on Bathtub Row where all the big shots live, and when I was walking home this MP stuck his flashlight in my face and asked to see my pass!"

"You're kidding!"

Kathy shakes her head. "Nope. And you know what I found out? They patrol all around the director's house, twenty-four hours a day. And around the houses of some of the other scientists who live up there, too. What do you think of *that?*"

I think it makes Mom not telling me the name of her boss seem like small potatoes. I finish writing all that down, and then I ask, "Is your dad at home, Kathy?"

"Of course not. He's at work."

"But he's here on the Hill? You're sure he isn't away somewhere?" I ask.

Kathy gives me that look of hers and says, "As of half an hour ago, he wasn't away. What are you getting at, anyhow?"

"Well, Dad didn't show up for breakfast this morning, and Mom said he'd gone someplace. All she'd tell me is that it has something to do with his work. I was just wondering if anybody else was gone."

Kathy says, "I'll bet we can find out."

I repack my knapsack, and as we leave for school I think that things are looking better already.

All day, I try to think of a way to find out where Dad could have gone off to, but no luck. I'm turning the whole thing over in my mind again at the end of math class when I hear Gail asking Mrs. James to explain one of the problems on last night's homework. My first thought is, *She should have asked her father.* My second thought is, *Gail's father must be away.*

I take my time copying the assignment and packing up my stuff so I can leave the classroom at the same time Gail does. "How come you didn't ask your dad for help with the homework?" I ask, holding the door for her.

"I usually do, but he's been away a lot lately."

Bingo! "My dad's away, too. I wonder if they've gone to the same place."

"All I know is, Daddy always comes back really tired. And sunburned."

Sunburned! Then they must be working outdoors. And this isn't the first time her father's been away. What the heck is going on?

Everybody's sort of milling around, waiting for the Sunday hike to start, and I'm trying not to be too obvious as I look around to see if any of the scientists who usually go on these outings are missing.

Kathy comes up to me and asks, "How come your knapsack looks so flat?"

"I took out everything but the Secret Project notebook so I'd have room to bring back rocks." I can see that she doesn't get it, so I explain. "Today's outing is to a ghost town, right? That means there's going to be a mine, 'cause that's why the town grew up there in the first place. And *that* means I'm going to find a lot of neat rocks for my collection. Rocks with minerals in them. Maybe even gold."

"If I ever decide to start a collection, I guarantee it won't be anything heavy," Kathy says. "How much longer are we going to stand around here before we start the hike?"

One of the little kids is whining, and I hear his mother say, "Jesse's been like this ever since his daddy left on Friday. Clingy and whiny and not sleeping at all well."

Bingo! "His dad's one of the disappearing fathers, Kath."

She shushes me, and I shut up in time to hear another woman saying, "—the same way last week when her dad was gone. She's hardly let him out of her sight since he came back."

"We need to find out who those fathers are," I whisper.

"Leave it to me," Kathy whispers back.

The hike leader hollers for everybody's attention, warns us to be alert for rattlesnakes and scorpions, and then sets off with everybody kind of strung out behind him. I watch Kathy go over to the two whiny kids and offer each of them a hand. They all go skipping off together, and I realize Kathy's going to find out the last names of those disappearing scientists by talking to their kids.

I stoop to double-knot my shoelaces, then sprint

ahead so I can walk with Dad. As I pass a trio of scientists I hear the words "just back from the Trinity site." *Bingo*, again! Hope I'm as lucky with my rock collecting.

"I'm glad you got back in time to come today, Dad," I say when I catch up to him.

"I'm glad, too, Fritz. I needed a break."

He sounds sort of grim, so I ask, "Is the project coming along okay?"

"It's coming along very well, Fritz. How are things at school? Is your math student still making progress?"

How's that for changing the subject? "Manny's doing really well," I tell him. "And now that Mrs. Evans makes him stay after school twice a week to work on his writing, he's doing better in English class, too."

"Mrs. Evans must think he has 'po-TEN-tial,'" Dad says.

Before I can answer, Kathy bounces up to join us—without the little kids—and Dad excuses himself to walk with two of the younger scientists.

"Get out your notebook before I forget these names," Kathy whispers.

I do as she says, figuring that people are used to seeing me writing in my Flora and Fauna notebook. They'll probably think I've found some interesting cactus or something. The names Kathy gives me are already on my Personnel list, so I put a "D" for *Disappearing* in parentheses beside both of them. Then I turn to the section on Codes, which is still pretty short, and write: "Trinity site—the place the scientists disappear to."

Kathy frowns and says, "Trinity? Maybe the

name's a clue to where it is. Maybe it's near three of something."

"Probably not," I say as I put my notebook away and shoulder the knapsack again. "Fat Man isn't a fat man, after all, and Little Boy isn't—"

"*Okay*, Fritz. It was just a thought."

"At least you were right when you bet that we'd be able to find out who was disappearing. But I still wonder where the heck they disappear to. Hey, look up ahead—I can see the entrance to the mine. Let's go!"

I'm sprawled on my bed, reviewing for a social studies quiz and thinking how unfair it is to schedule a test for Monday, when Kathy knocks. I know it's Kathy, 'cause nobody else comes to the door this early.

"Where's your notebook?" she asks.

I bring it to the kitchen table and find the Rumors and Observations pages.

Kathy leans toward me and says, "They go by car. The disappearing fathers. I woke up when a car door slammed in the middle of the night, and about a minute later, Daddy came in. I told you he was away, remember?"

Bingo! "You know what that means, Kathy? Car pools, that's what, 'cause your car was here while he was gone, right? This is great news, Kath!"

She frowns. "It is?"

"Sure—it means everybody's going to have a turn to drive." I can tell she still doesn't get it, so I explain. "Look, all we have to do is check the odometer before one of our dads drives the car pool and again after he comes back, and we'll know how far away this place is."

"But we never know when they're going, and even if we did, how would we know whose turn it was to drive?"

She has a point. "We'll have to keep track of the mileage," I tell her, "but that shouldn't be too hard. It's not like anybody does all that much driving, between gas rationing and working six days a week plus all that overtime. Write down the mileage this afternoon and check the odometer again if your parents go to Santa Fe or drive the car pool for an outing."

I bend over my notebook, and while Kathy watches, I write: "Kathy has discovered that the disappearing fathers travel to their mysterious destination by car pool."

"It's about time I got a little credit," she says. "Hey, look at the clock—we'd better go."

Holy cow! I cram the notebook into my knapsack and follow Kath out the door.

"So what did you think of the pueblo, Mom?" I ask as we drive up the mesa.

"I liked seeing the Indian people in their own environment instead of ours. It felt strange, though, to be in a place that's so—well, so timeless."

She slows and shifts to a lower gear as we approach a hairpin curve. When we're safely around it, I say, "I think Grandma's going to like that bowl you bought for her birthday. Be sure to tell her we know the potter."

This is the first time I've been inside Juanita's house, so I have a lot of things to write in Notes on Modern American Indians, like how benches and things were built right into those thick adobe walls and covered with hand-woven rugs or blankets. And I'll have to describe that beehive-shaped adobe oven out front where Juanita was baking bread. I'll have to find out if she fires her pottery there, too.

The car slows as we come to the main gate, and Mom and I get out our passes while we wait our turn to go in. "Hey, Mom! How come that MP is checking the trunk of the car ahead of us?" I'm not surprised when she doesn't bother to answer, but it makes me feel kind of foolish. Mostly, though, I feel curious. Does Security think something—or maybe some-*body*—is being smuggled in?

Now Mom's rolling down her window and show-ing our passes, and I try not to look like a kid whose Secret Project notebook is in his knapsack on the back seat. I concentrate on not thinking about my knapsack, just in case the MP's some kind of mind reader. Instead I think, *Hurry up and look in the trunk.*

Mom hands back my pass, and the guard goes around to check the trunk. But I don't breathe easily until he slams it shut and waves us through the gate.

We're driving past the trailer area—which is a heck of a lot larger than it was when we first got here—when something slams against the window on my side of the car. Mom hits the brake, and the car skids on the unpaved road. "Somebody threw a dirtball, Mom," I tell her. Craning my neck, I look back and see a bunch of kids dodge behind a parked truck—mostly little kids, but one of them was a scrawny red-haired boy about my age.

Mom starts in about kids running wild here on the mesa, but I don't listen. I'm too busy figuring out that Red was throwing dirtballs at *cars*, not at Fritz

Madden, so if I keep my mouth shut, he'll never have the satisfaction of knowing whose car he hit. Let somebody else sic the MPs on him—there can't be that many red-headed boys in the trailer camp.

When we get back to the apartment, I say, "Listen, Mom, I'll wash the dirt off the car window while you wrap that pottery bowl you got for Grandma." I brush away her thanks because I'm not doing it to be helpful. The truth is, it's a good chance for me to check the odometer and write down the mileage.

Wait till I tell Kathy how easy it was.

Chapter Eighteen

They closed the Lab when the news came—and that's really something, considering that it was business as usual on New Year's Day. But most people here on the Hill liked President Roosevelt, and everybody's pretty upset that he's died.

A couple of Dad's friends from work are here, talking in hushed voices, the way people do when somebody's "passed away." I figure that since I can't catch much of what they're saying when I'm here in the kitchen, the old glass trick won't work this time. Mom's brewed a pot of coffee, and I watch her fill the cups and put them on a tray. "Want me to carry that in there for you?"

"That's very thoughtful of you, hon," she says.

Actually, it's very sneaky of me because I'm hoping it will give me a chance to hear what's being said out there. I know Mom would just set the tray on the coffee table and leave, but I pass it around, waiting while each of the guys takes a cup and helps himself to cream and sugar. Trouble is, now they aren't talking.

I'm taking the tray back when Mom heads down the hall toward the bedrooms. Good. That means I'll be able to listen from right inside the kitchen doorway, which puts me a little closer than when I was sitting at the table.

By straining my ears I manage to catch a couple

of phrases: "Roosevelt's program . . . what if Truman doesn't . . . millions of dollars . . . maybe billions by the time . . . don't think they can very well abandon . . . we've come so far . . . ."

Hey, it sounds like they're worried that the new president might close this place down. Won't he want the scientists to finish their project and end the war? Desperate for a chance to hear what the men are saying, I rip open a package of cookies and arrange most of them on a plate to pass around. Then I go back for the coffee pot and hover respectfully a little bit away from them, so if they notice me they'll think I'm coming to fill the cups again.

A good plan, but it has two flaws. (1) The cups are still pretty full, and (2) Dad sees me and says, "I don't think we'll be needing anything else, Fritz."

Since that's his polite way of telling me to get lost, I take the pot back to the kitchen, grab a couple of broken cookies I didn't put on the plate, and head for my room. I turn to Rumors and Observations in my Secret Project notebook and write: "April 12, 1945— President Franklin D. Roosevelt's death raises the question of whether the secret project, which has come so far and has cost millions and perhaps billions of dollars, will be continued under President Harry Truman."

I read it over and think it sounds almost as good as the *Denver Post.* And then I wonder how reporters ever get enough information to write one of those long articles when it took me about an hour to get enough for a sentence.

***

The afternoon sun makes the drifts of spring snow sparkle as Kathy and I trudge along behind our parents on the way home from President Roosevelt's memorial service. "You're going to have to help me remember what the director said about the president, Kathy—the *late* president, that would be—because I'm going to start a new notebook as soon as I get home," I tell her. "I'll call this one History as I Experienced It, and I'm going to start it with the day Roosevelt died. I'll tell about how shocked everybody was, almost like they thought that because he'd been president for so long he always would be. I'll put what the director said at the service in my concluding paragraph, and— Hey, there's Jacob and his dad getting off that bus."

"And they've got their skis," Kathy says, sounding envious.

"Hey, Jacob!" I holler. "You missed the memorial service for the president."

Jacob hesitates a moment before he calls, "We did not plan to attend."

Wishing I'd kept my big mouth shut, I call back, "See you at school tomorrow."

Kathy and I hurry to catch up to our parents. They're waiting for us at the corner, and Mom asks, "What was all that about, Fritz?"

"Nothing. I was just mentioning to Jacob that he and his father missed the memorial service."

Dad frowns and says, "Roosevelt isn't—wasn't— Hermann's favorite person."

My ears perk up. "How come?"

"Because he thinks FDR could have done more to help the Jews, son." Dad hesitates a moment before he adds, "Some of Hermann's relatives were on a refugee ship that was turned away by the U.S. after Cuba refused to let the people ashore even though they'd been given visas."

"So where did they go?"

"Back to Europe, after other countries in this hemisphere wouldn't take them in, either."

Those photos of concentration camp survivors flash into my mind, and I force myself to ask, "Do you think they ended up in the death camps?"

Dad sighs and says, "One assumes that a good many of them did, Fritz."

No wonder Jacob and his father didn't go to the memorial service! "How come we wouldn't help them? Didn't we know what would happen if we didn't?"

We walk a few more steps before Dad says, "I don't think anyone had a crystal ball, son."

I get the message and stop asking questions. The wind rises and blows a cloud of powdery snow along the street, then drops and the snow falls into small dunes. Somehow, watching that makes me feel incredibly sad.

Chapter Nineteen

"Dad's gone *again*?"

"Yes," Mom says, sitting down at the table, "and don't bother to ask me when he'll be back, because I don't know any more than you do. I just get up and fix his breakfast and send him off at 3:00 a.m. with a thermos of coffee and a bag lunch."

I make a mental note of the time he leaves so I can write it down later. You never know what little piece of information might turn out to be an important clue.

"So what are your plans for the day?" Mom asks, sounding a little less crabby now. "You're up early for a Saturday."

"Going riding with Manny again now that the snow's melted. He said we'd explore one of the smaller canyons."

After breakfast, I pack my lunch and leave. I'm almost to the bottom of the steps when I stop short—*our car is gone.* Wait till I tell Kathy that Dad drove the disappearing fathers' car pool! Now all we have to do is wait till he comes home, and we'll know how far they go, 'cause nobody drove anywhere since I wrote down the mileage.

I'm still pretty excited about this when I get to the stable. Manny isn't there yet, but I head for the tack room for Brownie's saddle and bridle. By the time

I've got her ready to go, Manny still hasn't shown up. It's not like him to be late. I'm wondering if I should go ahead and saddle Coal Dust, when this little kid comes running up.

When he catches his breath, he says, "My brother, he don't feel so good. He says for you to go without him."

I thank the kid for coming to tell me and reward him with the chocolate bar I'd packed in my lunch. Since I'm not about to go exploring on my own, I decide to ride down the bridle trail into the main canyon and see what's blooming at the lower elevations, where it's warmer.

The trail's on sort of a ledge, and it leads down the slope in a series of switch-back turns. About halfway down, I start to see tiny flowering plants clinging to the rocks, so I stop and reach into my knapsack for *Wildflowers of the Southwest.* What I'm trying to identify doesn't look much like any of the pictures in the book, so I jot down a description and go on.

I have better luck down on the canyon floor and add a couple more new plants to Notes on Flora and Fauna before I decide to have a snack. I'm sitting on a rock by the stream, enjoying the last of my oatmeal cookies, when I see something that makes me lose my appetite: Lonny and Red, walking along the stream with their fishing poles. They haven't seen me yet, but they're coming this way.

I'm wrong—they've seen me, and now they're walking faster. I shrug on my knapsack and dash over to Brownie. Grab the pommel of the saddle. Put a foot in the stirrup. Sling my other leg over. They're running toward me now. Lonny's close enough I can see his sneering face, and Red's right behind him.

I wheel Brownie around, dig in my heels, and head back the way we came. A rock whizzes past my right ear, and another lands a few feet ahead on my left. Uh-oh. Snowballs and dirtballs are one thing, but rocks— One bounces off the heel of my boot, and then Brownie gives a start, so I figure she's been hit. Now I'm mad as well as scared, but there's nothing I can do except get the two of us out of here.

When we finally come to the beginning of the switchback trail, I rein Brownie in. I know Lonny and Red can't possibly catch up, but my heart's pounding like I was the one doing the running.

All the way back, I've got one thing on my mind: I'd better make sure those two never get hold of me like they almost did back there. That they never find me off somewhere by myself. 'Cause the truth is, without Manny or Jacob to stick up for me, I'm a sitting duck. Or maybe a dead one, considering how much damage those two did to me right out in public.

Worrying about being beat up is bad enough, but the worst thing is knowing I'm a coward. A sissy. And knowing that Lonny and Red—not to mention Kathy, Manny, and Jacob—know that as well as I do.

I wake up with the feeling that something's wrong, and then I remember—it's Monday, the day Lonny and Red are going to start making my life miserable again. I sure hope Manny's at school to run interference.

But when I slip into my first period class, Manny's seat is empty. Why the heck is he always absent when I need him? I feel a dull ache in my stomach, but then I remind myself that it's not school I have to worry about. Those goons can't do anything to me unless they get me alone, and I'm going to make sure that doesn't happen.

I manage to avoid them all day, and after school I stop by the library and browse through a couple of references, trying to find a picture of that plant I saw in the canyon—and to give those two time to clear out before I take Manny his math homework. Still can't identify that plant I saw Saturday. Oh, well. Better get on with my errand. I check Manny's address on the manila envelope Mrs. James put his work in, and then I set off.

When I get to the Quonset hut area, I clomp along one of the wooden sidewalks that lead between the rows of huts, outlining rectangular patches of bare ground that can hardly be called yards.

This whole place is really geometric. My eyes move from the vertical lines of smokestacks, clothesline poles, and power line poles to the horizontal lines of the ropes and wires strung between the poles. And then I look at the Quonset huts themselves, rising between the board sidewalks. I study the prefab buildings as I pass them—arched metal structures that look sort of like long cylinders lying half buried in the dirt. Living in one of those must feel like being inside a tunnel.

I walk past a building marked Bath House, and I'm so busy gawking I forget to check the numbers on the huts and almost pass the one where Manny lives. I knock at the door, and while I'm waiting for someone to come, I notice that the small front windows have white curtains, neatly tied back to let in more light, and that the glass panes are sparkling clean. With all the dust in this place, somebody must be washing those windows just about every day.

Finally the door opens, and an old woman peers out at me. "Does Manny live here?" I ask, figuring she must be his grandmother. She says something in Spanish, and all I can understand is "Si, Manny, si," but I figure that's enough, so I hand her the homework assignments and say, "For Manny." She takes the manila envelope and when she says "Gracias," I wish I knew the Spanish words for "You're welcome."

I clomp back along the boardwalk, slowing for a better look at this run-down place I passed on my way in. Beer bottles litter the front yard, and an army-issue kitchen chair with a broken seat lies on its side, baked into the dried mud. I'm looking at the dish towels hung haphazardly across the front windows instead of curtains, wondering how anybody can live like that, when the door bursts open—and I'm looking at Lonny.

I don't wait to hear what he's yelling at me. I sprint along the boardwalk, dodge a lady carrying a bag of groceries, and don't slow down till I get to the main road. My heart's thumping against my ribs, and I'm gasping for breath, and here come a couple little girls from the lower school, licking lollipops. One of them asks, "What was you runnin' like that for?"

"Practicing for the big race," I lie.

"At school?" she asks, looking interested.

I shake my head. "In Santa Fe." I glance behind me to make sure Lonny isn't coming after me, and then I head toward the PX to buy Dad's paper. At least I know Lonny isn't over there, and without Lonny to back him up, Red is mostly mouth.

137

Since I'm not in any hurry, I read all the way through the latest Batman comic before I get in line to pay for my newspaper. I'm standing here, listening to the jukebox playing "Don't Fence Me In," when somebody walking past jostles my arm and says, "Fritz the Fraidy Cat."

What the heck—? I thought he was back where he lives. My heartbeat speeds up. Did Lonny come looking for me, or was he already planning to spend some time over here?

"Fritz the Fraidy Cat." This time, he says it louder, and bumps against me harder. He looks back over his shoulder at me, and the mixture of scorn and triumph on his face makes me feel like some kind of insect. Reminding myself that I'm in a crowded, brightly lit place, I step out of line and go after him. Just as he reaches out to take a comic book off the rack, I grab his arm. "Listen here, Lonny, if you don't lay off me, I'm gonna to tell everybody you live in a pig pen."

He scowls and says, "It ain't nobody's business how I live."

"You're right. Leave me alone, and you can keep it that way. It's up to you."

He shakes my hand off his arm—I didn't realize I still had hold of him—and heads toward the pinball machines. I start back to the end of the line, hoping nobody notices I'm trembling. Halfway there, some enlisted guy stops me and says, "Here, kid. I saved your place for you."

I thank him and step back in line, feeling kind of proud of myself for a change. I'm not dumb enough to think confronting Lonny a minute ago is really going to make him lay off me, but it's better than letting him get away with calling me names. And it's a heck of a lot better than running away from him.

I've got to get out of here the instant math class is over, before Mrs. James can ask me to take Manny his homework again today. I swallow hard and try not to think of what Lonny said this morning when he passed my desk in social studies class: You'll stay off my territory if you know what's good for you, Fritz Madden.

The minute Mrs. Evans dismisses us, I burst into the hall, almost crashing into Jacob. He takes one look at me and says, "They are bothering you again."

"Sort of," I admit.

Before I can say more, Mrs. James comes out of the classroom. "I'm glad I caught you, Fritz," she says. "Here's Manny's homework."

I feel my shoulders sag and wonder if Jacob could have noticed, because he asks, "Is this Manny another of the bullies?"

"He's my friend. He's absent, and I'm supposed to take him his homework, but he lives in the same neighborhood as Lonny."

Jacob frowns fiercely and says, "You must not allow this Lonny to keep you from helping a friend. Wait for me after school, and we will go together."

I feel a rush of relief and then a long, slow build-up of shame. Partly for being a coward, partly for almost letting down somebody who's counting on me.

After school Jacob is waiting for me outside the building, and we set off together. He doesn't seem to want to talk, and I wonder if that's because he doesn't have much use for Fritz the Fraidy Cat or because he's preoccupied.

As we approach the neighborhood of Quonset huts, Jacob says, "I would not wish to live in this place."

"It makes pretty much anywhere else seem luxurious in comparison," I agree. "Where do you live?"

"We were assigned to what they called a prefab duplex. Its walls are the thickness of cardboard, so we hear every word of the family next door, and they hear every word of ours. They, however, cannot understand our words as we can theirs."

"Our walls are thin, too. All our neighbors have little kids who make a lot of noise, and the man downstairs plays Mozart and Beethoven on his record player every night."

Jacob says, "You are fortunate. Our neighbor plays jazz." He says "jazz" the way Vivian would have said "spider."

Manny's place is just ahead, and the old lady is in the yard, taking laundry off the clothesline. Her basket is almost full, but there's still a row of plaid flannel shirts, some medium-sized, some small. She turns around when she hears our footsteps echo on the wooden sidewalk, and her face lights up with recognition. She hurries toward the door, but instead of going inside, she picks up something from the doorstep—a manila envelope. Yesterday's homework. *Manny was expecting me. What if I hadn't come?*

The old lady and I trade envelopes, smile, and each of us says something in our own language before Jacob and I start back. "On your right is where Lonny lives," I say as we're passing his place, and Jacob mutters something that sounds like "swine."

We're almost to the road when I spot Lonny and Red walking toward us.

"I see you brought your bodyguard with you," Lonny hollers. "You think that gives you the right to come over here after I told you to stay away?"

"I can come here anytime I want, with or without my bodyguard," I holler back. "Wanna make something of it?" I've always wanted to say that, and with the Human Tornado right next to me, I finally can. The two of us keep on walking, and so do Lonny and Red. The distance between us narrows, but nobody shows any signs of slowing down. I grit my teeth and force myself to keep up with Jacob until everybody stops at once. We're about three feet apart.

Lonny gives me a scornful look and says, "You're a lot braver when you've got somebody along to fight your battles for you, Fritzy-Witzy."

"And *you're* a lot braver when you've got somebody along to fight your battles *with* you, Lonny-Wonny."

We stand there glaring at each other until Jacob says quietly, "You will please stand aside so we may pass," and like some kind of magic, Lonny steps off one side of the boardwalk and Red steps off the other side. The two of us walk between them, and I can feel their eyes boring into my back as we continue out to the road.

"That was almost like the parting of the Red Sea!" I marvel once we're out of hearing distance.

Jacob laughs, and for a minute he looks like any other fourteen-year-old kid instead of the Human Tornado. "Lonny-Wonny, you called him! You dare to mock him even though you fear him?"

"Like he said, my bodyguard was with me. Besides,

I'm a lot better with words than I am with my fists."

The sparkle goes out of Jacob's eyes, and he says quietly, "When one is pushed far enough, one's fists sometimes take on a life of their own."

Not mine. "I have to stop by the PX for my dad's newspaper," I say. "Thanks for going over to Manny's with me."

Jacob shrugs off my thanks and says, "Perhaps you would like to play a game of ping-pong if a table at the PX is available?"

"That would be great! I've got to warn you, though—I'm not an outstanding player." Fritzy-Witzy versus the Human Tornado.

"I will give you a large handicap, and then I will teach you to be an outstanding player."

The way he said that, it sounded as much like a threat as a promise, but I figure it doesn't much matter. What matters is that Jacob wants to be friends.

Manny shoves his math make-up test under my nose and says, "Look at this, would ya?"

"Hey, that's great," I tell him. "I'll bet your dad's going to be proud."

Manny's face clouds over. "We ain't seen him for so long I doubt my baby sister remembers what he looks like."

Something clicks in my memory. That's why there were only small and medium-sized shirts on the clothesline the last time I took Manny his homework! "Your dad's gone? You're lucky they haven't made your family move off the Hill."

"Not *that* kind of gone, Fritz." Manny looks shocked at the idea. "They loaded him and a lot of other workers on a bus a while back, and that's the last we seen of 'em. Boy I play ball with, his pa saw a busload of MPs leavin' the mesa, and that was even longer ago. Pedro's father—he's a carpenter—was gone for a while, but he's back now."

Holy cow! I'd thought it was only the scientists who were disappearing. "What the heck's going on, Manny?"

"Don't know and probably never will. They ain't supposed to say nothing about what they're building, you know. Guys that talk don't last very long around here."

That sounds pretty sinister until I realize Manny means they're fired. "Well, save that math test to show your dad when he finally comes back."

"Yeah," Manny agrees, carefully folding the paper and putting it in his math book. "Guess this means I can graduate myself from you helping me after school."

"Guess so, Manny." I'm a little relieved not to be tied up three afternoons a week now that I'm playing ping-pong with Jacob, but I try not to let on.

Manny says, "I'll still show you the old Indian ruins and stuff like that, but not as a favor anymore. Just as something we do together, okay?"

"Sure," I say. "That would be great." Actually, I hadn't thought of our math sessions and Saturday rides as "favors" for a long time.

We go outside, and without being real obvious about it, Manny checks to make sure Lonny and Red aren't hanging around, and then we say good-bye. I head toward home, wishing I could "graduate myself" from being intimidated by goons like them.

Chapter Twenty

I wake up early even though it's Sunday. After I get dressed I wander into the living room to look out at the mountains, like I always do, and before I turn away from the window I glance down and see that our car's parked in its usual spot again. Hot dog! That means two things: (1) Dad's back, and (2) I can check the odometer and figure out how far away the disappearing fathers go.

A pencil. Paper. Open the door without making a sound. Tiptoe across the balcony and down the steps. Walk toward the car.

I'm reaching for the door handle when Dad shouts, *"Franklin!"* I freeze. "Come back here, Franklin."

I half trot back to the building and up the steps, even though I'd much rather be running in the opposite direction. "Welcome home, Dad. What's the matter?"

He takes me by the arm and says. "Get inside. You're going to be answering questions, not asking them." This is the angriest I've ever seen him, but he'd look a lot scarier if he weren't barefooted and wearing striped pajamas.

"What were you up to, sneaking around the car at this hour of the morning?"

I swallow hard. "I woke up early, and when I saw the car I knew you were home, so I— Well, I thought I'd go out and look at the car."

"With a piece of paper and a pencil?"

"Um, yeah. I guess."

Dad doesn't say anything, but I can feel his eyes on me. I keep staring down at the floor, waiting for him to say something else, but he doesn't. I start to feel warm, like maybe the heat of his gaze is making me melt. How come he doesn't say anything? Yell at me?

I hear the whispery sound of Mom's slippers as she comes down the hall. The sound stops, and she says, "What on earth is going on in here, Verne?"

"I found your son outside, Mona. Snooping around the car. I'm waiting for him to tell me what he was up to and why he had paper and pencil with him."

Mom has this puzzled expression as she looks from Dad to me and back to Dad again. "Have you asked him?"

"I have, and he did not give a satisfactory answer."

"Dad's acting like he thinks I'm a spy or something, Mom." Now that he's looking at her instead of me, I don't feel as much like one of those butterfly specimens with a pin through it.

Mom says, "I can't deal with this before I've had my coffee," and she disappears into the kitchen, leaving me at Dad's mercy.

"I know you aren't a spy, Fritz," Dad says, running his fingers through his hair, "but that doesn't change the fact that you were snooping around the car just after I returned from a trip that requires the highest level of security. I need to know what you expected to find out. What you intended to write down. And why."

Dad—or else Mom—will get it out of me eventually, so I might as well save us all some time. "I was planning to look at the odometer and write down the mileage."

"And what were you planning to do with that information?"

Dad's using his no-nonsense tone, so I've got to tell him. "I was going to subtract what the mileage was before you left and divide the answer by two so I'd know how far away you go when you disappear."

Dad runs his fingers through his hair again and asks, "How do you happen to know what the mileage was before I left when you had no idea that I was going, much less that I would be driving?"

I stare down at the floor and don't answer. If I tell him, I'll have to explain about my Secret Project notebook, and then he'll insist on seeing it, and *then* he'll confiscate it.

"Fritz, I asked you a question."

I glance up at him long enough to see that he looks stern now rather than angry, and then I stare at the floor again and say, "I refuse to answer on the grounds that I might incriminate myself."

"That only works in a court of law, Franklin. It does not work with me. I want an answer. Now."

"He's bluffing, Verne," Mom says from the kitchen doorway. "Don't make an issue of this."

I'm about to say that I can tell them exactly what the mileage was before Dad's trip, but I catch myself in time.

"Mona, if security has been lax enough that a schoolboy is aware of our comings and goings—"

"I don't know anything about your comings and goings, Dad. I don't know anything at all—honest!" It's all rumors and observations.

Mom says, "Keep in mind what you are dealing with here, Verne—a bright and very imaginative youngster who reads spy thrillers."

I hold my breath until finally Dad says, "Maybe you're right, Mona. Is that coffee ready yet?" Mom goes back to the kitchen, and Dad turns to me. "Listen, son," he says. "What I'm involved in here is serious business, and I mean life-and-death serious. Nothing can be allowed to jeopardize this project. Do you understand?"

"I understand, Dad." I don't want to jeopardize the project. I just want to know what it's all about.

"Is it okay if we stay for a couple minutes to look at one of your maps?" I ask Mrs. Jackson after class.

"Sure. Just pull the door shut when you leave." Kathy has already found the map that shows geographical features. "Mountains pretty much everywhere around here except along the Rio Grande Valley," she muses.

"Yes, but look there to the south. The valley widens out, and it's not nearly as rugged."

"It's not too close to Santa Fe or Albuquerque, either," Kathy says. "That's got to be where our fathers go when they disappear. See? We didn't need to check their odometers to find out. We should have thought to look at the map in the first place—it would have saved us a lot of trouble."

I'd still like to know something more specific than "south of here," so I'm not as elated as Kathy seems to be. Still, by the time we pull the door shut behind us, I'm already planning what I'll say under Rumors and Observations. Lunch will have to wait.

As soon as I get home I take my notebook out of my knapsack and begin to write. "On the New Mexico desert some distance south of Santa Fe, scientists from the Hill are—"

Are *what?*

I erase all that and start over. "When the scientists disappear from the laboratory and their homes, they are probably traveling some distance to the south to another secret location to continue their secret work." Don't I know anything more than that? I close my eyes and concentrate, trying to think if there's a clue I might have missed. *Bingo!* "This location is guarded by military police and contains numerous wooden structures." Structures built by Pedro's father, among others. I change that period to a comma and add, "some of which are barracks." All those MPs and scientists have to sleep somewhere, don't they?

Chapter Twenty-One

Jacob and I are going into the PX for our usual ping-pong session when a couple of GIs come out, cheering and hollering. One of them holds the door for us and says, "You kids heard the news yet? He's dead! That #!@*#! Hitler's dead—killed himself in his bunker."

I'm slipping off my knapsack to get out my new *History as I Experienced* notebook when I notice that Jacob has gotten very still. "What's the matter? Aren't you glad he's dead?"

"Better that he was never born," Jacob says, and his voice is so shaky that I drop the subject real fast and head toward the ping-pong table, adjusting my knapsack as I go.

A couple of soldiers are already playing, and when one of them calls out the score I realize they've just started a new game. Still, I'm surprised when Jacob says, "If you do not mind, Fritz, I will go home now instead of waiting for our turn at the table."

When I see how pale he looks, I realize he must still be thinking about Hitler, or something. "Sure," I say. "See you tomorrow, then." I watch the guys play for a while, and then I hang around the newspaper stand and write down what people say when they see the headline about Hitler.

I get home in time to hear Dad say, "—beginning of the end. Now the generals can surrender without fearing for their lives at the hands of that madman."

"I guess once the Germans surrender, you won't have to go back to the Lab after dinner anymore. Right, Dad?"

Dad shakes his head. "The Germans have been out of the picture for some time now, as far as the project is concerned, Fritz."

"But I thought the whole idea was that our scientists were racing against theirs to—"

"Fritz."

He's using that no-nonsense tone on me again. "Okay, Dad." If Security is listening in on any microphones hidden around here, they're wasting their time.

"Don't take it so hard, kiddo. The important thing is that the war in Europe is almost over. Then we'll be able to concentrate on beating the Japanese."

I guess that means that instead of racing to beat the Germans, now they're racing to end the war as soon as possible.

I'm so stuffed I can hardly move, but like Mom says, feasting is as good a way as any to celebrate the end of the war in Europe. I look through my notebooks, pull out History as I Experienced It, and begin to write: "May 8,1945. V-E Day. The Germans have surrendered, and Americans are celebrating. Here on the Hill, little kids marched around beating on pots and pans, and some of the grown-ups got drunk."

I turn the page and continue: "Our building and the one next door had a big potluck supper, and we could hear car horns blaring and loud music coming from the army barracks and from the dormitories where the unmarried scientists live. Dad and a lot of the other men were missing, away at the secret place where scientists keep disappearing to. The men who were at the supper left early to go back to their labs."

When I said it was too bad they had to leave, Mom said, "Don't kid yourself, Fritz. There isn't a scientist on this mesa who wouldn't rather work than eat," and Timmy's mother added, "I used to feel sorry for Greg, having to work late every night. Then I realized he loved having an excuse to go back to the Lab."

I'm thinking about this when I hear some kind of commotion outside. I go to the window but don't see anything, so I raise the sash and listen. It's whooping and cheering, against the background of a relentless drumbeat.

I grab the Indian blanket off my bed, wrap it around my shoulders, and kneel by the open window, peering into the night as the sound grows louder. There they come—it's a conga line! Snaking along the dark street is a long, noisy column of dancers, each with hands on the waist of the person in front, and all more or less keeping time to the pounding drum— One, Two, Three, KICK! One, Two, Three, KICK!

Finally the end of the column passes, but I don't close the window till the sound dies away. Still wrapped in my blanket, I open Notes on the Secret Project to the Rumors and Observations pages and write: "Now that the Germans have surrendered, whatever the scientists are working on will be used against the Japanese. I know this because broadcasts from a sound truck that drove along the streets blared out the message that people 'must not slack in their efforts' now that the war is over in Europe because the Japanese must still be defeated."

151

For once, Mrs. Jackson doesn't ask anybody what they think is the most significant news article, 'cause it's so obvious. And for once, Kathy and Gail and the other girls don't seem to mind talking about the war. In fact, Kathy has a lot to say about it. She's really excited that the war's over in Europe and Matthew's safe.

To tell the truth, we're all pretty excited. Everybody's talking about how they felt when they first heard the news and how relieved they are that the Germans finally surrendered. For once I'm paying attention, 'cause I figure I can use a lot of this in my History As I Experienced It notebook.

Good grief. Kathy's talking again. "In a way, though, V-E Day was kind of an anticlimax for me," she says, "'cause Mom and I celebrated last week when the German army in Italy surrendered. We had a steak dinner at the Lodge," she adds, as if anybody would care.

"How come you celebrated when they surrendered in Italy?" Manny asks.

"'Cause that's where my brother was fighting, and it meant we didn't have to worry any longer about him being killed. It was such a relief to know he wasn't in danger anymore. To know that he'd be coming home soon," Kathy explains. "That meant a lot more to me than V-E Day did."

For a couple of seconds, everybody's either staring at Kathy with shocked expressions on their faces, or else studying the tops of their desks because they're embarrassed for her. I mostly study my desktop, but

I can't help glancing around to see how the other kids are taking it.

Dietrich, who's hardly opened his mouth all year says, "A whole continent is finally at peace—no more bombing and destruction of cities, no more slaughter on the battlefield, no more murder of Jews in the camps—and all it means to Kathy is that now her brother is safe."

Gail speaks up to say, "I guess if we multiply Kathy's relief a couple million times, that's how the whole world is feeling right now."

Good for Gail. People start to talk again, but Kathy doesn't say anything more for the rest of period, so I guess she's feeling pretty bad.

Class finally ends, and I'm packing up my stuff when Red hollers, "Hey, Miz Jackson—Kathy's bawling." I look up just as he jostles past me, saying, "I sure am glad me and Lonny don't have no crybaby girlfriends."

I take all the stuff out of my knapsack and repack it, stalling to make sure the goons are gone before I start home. I'm buckling the straps when Gail stops at my desk and says, "Do you mind waiting to walk home with Kathy? I hate to leave her like this, but Mom took the bus to Santa Fe and I'm supposed to fix my little brother's lunch."

Gail leaves, and when I steal a look at Kathy, she's got her head down on the desk and Mrs. Jackson's patting her shoulder. I turn around and sit with my back to them, wishing I'd thought to tell Gail *I'd* fix her brother's lunch so *she* could stay here.

Finally, Mrs. Jackson says, "Fritz, are you waiting for Kathy?" Without looking around, I tell her I am, and pretty soon Kathy shuffles up and says she's ready to go. Boy, it's a good thing the other kids have left, 'cause she's a sight, all red and swollen. I'm glad I'll be walking next to her and won't have to look at her.

Kathy doesn't say anything on the way out of the building. All the way across the school yard, she doesn't say anything. I'm figuring it's going to be a long walk home when she says, "For the rest of their lives, whenever they think about V-E Day, everybody's going to remember what I said and what Dietrich said."

She's probably right, but something tells me I'd better not agree with her, so I try to think what Gail would say. "Come on, Kathy. There's nothing wrong with being relieved that Matthew's safe. Or about wanting to celebrate when you found out, either." The strange thing is, once I hear myself say it, I sort of believe it.

"You sound like Gail," Kathy says, wiping her eyes.

"You mean you didn't know she's a ventriloquist?"

Kathy manages a shaky laugh, and then she says, "Don't wait for me after lunch, Fritz, 'cause I'm not going back."

I think fast and say, "That's great! You'll get a zero for the day in math, and that means I won't have any competition for the highest average in the class."

"I hadn't thought about that," Kathy says, sounding more like she usually does.

We come to my building, and I say, "Well, see you tomorrow."

"You'll see me this afternoon, Fritz Madden," she calls after me. "I'm not going to let you walk away with the best average without putting up a fight."

I go up the stairs two at a time. Our next door neighbor is taking her laundry off the clothesline on the balcony, and she says, "Well, you're in good spirits today, Fritz."

"Must be the lingering effects of V-E Day," I tell her. That and knowing I just managed to say the absolutely right thing at the right time for probably the first time in my entire life.

Chapter Twenty-Two

I glance around the library and don't see anybody except juniors and seniors, but then I spot Kathy and Gail. At first I think they're doing their social studies report together, but when I sit down across from them it's easy to see it isn't school work. Looks more like a letter.

"Whatcha doing?" I whisper.

Gail quickly turns the paper over, but Kathy says, "Let him see—he'll get a kick out of it."

It's a letter, just like I thought. Actually, it's some kind of love letter, and I feel my face start to burn. I'm about to hand it back when I realize this has got to be a joke, so I go ahead and read it.

> Dear Harry,
>
> Each hour we are apart seems like a week, each day like a century. My eyes long to see you, my ears yearn to hear your voice, my lips perish for want of your kisses.

When I get to the end, I see that they've signed it Your Very Own Honey Bunch. As I hand it back, I whisper, "You'd better copy this onto some pink stationery before you send it." I'm joking, but the girls take me seriously.

Gail says, "I only have white paper, but I'm going

to spray it with my mom's perfume."

I can feel my eyebrows going north. "You're actually going to mail that? To who?"

"*Shh.* To a fake army post office box number in San Francisco," Kathy says, "like it's for some soldier in the Pacific. And it's 'to whom,' Fritz. Only owls say 'to who.'"

Gail starts to giggle, and I decide this is a good time for me to get some information for my social studies report. I leave the girls and spend the rest of the period taking notes from the encyclopedia.

As I start to leave, Gail calls for me to wait. "Don't tell your friend Jacob about our letter, okay?"

"I don't intend to tell anybody about it. But how come you don't want him to know?"

Gail turns a rosy pink color. "Because he'd think it's silly."

"He probably would—he's sort of serious, you know."

"He's such a tragic figure," Gail says dramatically. "And to think he's a friend of yours."

A tragic figure? "Listen, I'd better go."

Kathy calls, "Wait for me," and as we all leave the library together, Jacob walks past us without speaking. I figure he's having one of his gloomy, unsociable days, but Gail says, "He reminds me of the great English romantic poet, Lord Byron."

Before she can say anything else about romance or poetry, I ask, "Who's going to put that letter from Honey Bunch in the censors' box over in the Tech Area for you?"

"Kathy's mom works over there, and she'll drop it off for us like she has all the others," Gail says. "She

157

thinks I'm doing my patriotic duty by writing to soldier pen pals."

"We address each one to a different fake guy," Kathy explains.

"So how come you're doing this?" I ask as the three of us start home for lunch.

Gail shrugs. "Just for fun—and to amuse the censors."

"And to make them wonder," Kathy says with a wicked grin.

"Hey, I've got an idea that will *really* make them wonder," I tell her. "You could write a letter to the censor and complain that he must not have sent any of your letters, being as you haven't gotten a single answer."

Kathy's eyes light up, but Gail says, "There's only one problem with that. How do we explain to Kathy's mom why I'm writing a letter to the censor?"

"You won't have to. Start the letter with 'Dear Censor,' but address the envelope to another one of your fake boyfriends."

Kathy laughs. "Think how surprised that censor's going to be when he opens it and sees that it's to *him.*"

We say goodbye, and I dash upstairs to heat up some soup and fix a sandwich. While I'm eating, I wonder how the girls knew to write all that mushy stuff in their fake letter. And then I start looking forward to reading the one they'll write to the censor.

The minute Kathy walks into math class, I know something's wrong. I start to ask her what's the matter, but Gail shakes her head to signal me not to. A little later, she gets up to sharpen her pencil, so I wait a couple of seconds and go over to the sharpener with her.

"At lunch time Kathy's mom told her Matthew won't be coming home after all," Gail whispers. "He's being redeployed."

Redeployed? "You mean now they're going to send him to fight the Japanese?"

Gail nods. She takes a look at her pencil point and moves aside. "First he'll be retrained, and then they'll send him somewhere in the Pacific. Kathy asked me to tell you—she can't talk about it without crying." Gail's eyes fill with tears, and I start cranking the pencil sharpener.

I think about the fighting going on in the Pacific now, on the island of Okinawa. Fighting that's even worse than the Battle of Iwo Jima earlier this year. I read in the paper that the closer the fighting gets to the Japanese home islands, the worse it is.

"Fritz, don't you think that pencil is sharp enough now?" Mrs. James asks.

Actually, that pencil is just about gone now. I head back to my seat, hoping it takes a long time to retrain Matthew's unit. Hoping it takes so long that the war will be over before he's retrained, so he won't have to fight the Japanese.

Good grief. Now I'm thinking like Kathy does.

"Gail and I need your help with a technical problem regarding some correspondence," Kathy says, stopping by my desk after English class. "Okay?"

"Sure! You two work fast." She doesn't say anything about Matthew not coming home, and I'm not about to bring it up. I'm relieved to see that except for looking a little pale, she seems pretty much like her old self again.

We meet in the library after school, and Gail opens her three-ring binder and takes out a really messy rough draft.

Dear Censor,

And don't you pretend you're not reading this, because I know you are. In the last month, I have written to servicemen overseas and at bases in this country, and I demand to know why you haven't sent them my letters. And don't try to convince me that you did, because I haven't received a single answer, and men ALWAYS answer my letters. Don't try that "breach of security" excuse with me, either. These were love letters, and absolutely no security was breached.

"This is great!" I say, looking up. "What's the problem?"

Gail says, "We don't know how to sign it. We can't very well use Honey Bunch on a letter to the censor."

I think for a minute. "How about adding something like 'Many people here complain that their letters are not being received, so please respond to my question in *The Daily Bulletin.*' Then you can sign it Irate Postal Customer."

"And we can watch to see if the censor really answers it!" Kathy says. We all three shake hands, and then Gail writes down the final paragraph as I dictate it.

"When I copy this over, I'll use a little circle to dot each "i" instead of a heart like I usually do," Gail says.

"But use the little hearts when you address the envelope, so the censor will be expecting to find another steamy letter inside," I tell her.

Kathy sighs and says, "Wouldn't that be a nice way to spend the war—safe in an office somewhere, reading other people's mail? Why couldn't the army have given Matthew a job like that instead of sending him overseas?"

Mom's reading the mail when I come home from playing ping-pong with Jacob, and she passes me Vivian's letter. I glance through it even though I'm not really interested in much of anything my sister has to say. I'm almost to the end when Mom looks up from Grandma's letter and exclaims, "This is ridiculous! When Mother wrote this, she still hadn't gotten the letter I'd mailed her two weeks earlier! If Security is going to read all our correspondence, I certainly wish they'd read it faster."

"Maybe you ought to write a note to the censor and paperclip it to the envelope of the next letter you mail," I tell her. "You know—a note complaining about the delay."

"I believe I will, Fritz. In fact, I'll do it tonight."

Bingo! Wait till Kathy and Gail hear that my mom's going to add some credibility to their Irate Postal Customer's complaint.

Chapter Twenty-Three

A parade of little kids marches past the upper school door, chanting, "No more pencils, no more books," and I join in with "No more teachers' dirty looks."

Kathy makes that same *tsk* sound Mom does, and Gail says, "All I can think of is 'No yearbook, no eighth-grade dance.'" She sighs. "I know I've learned more in the upper school here than I would have in our junior high at home, but I hate missing out on all those traditions we're supposed to remember for the rest of our lives."

Traditions or not, I'll remember seventh grade for the rest of my life. I'm going to remember everything— and everybody.

"Are you sure Jacob's coming?" Gail asks as a bunch of rowdy older boys pass us, pushing and shoving each other as they leave the building. "You don't suppose he's already gone over to the PX, do you?"

"He said he'd meet us here," I tell her. It was Gail's idea for me to ask him to go with the three of us to celebrate the end of the school year. She didn't want Jacob to know that, but I figured he ought to know before he made up his mind, so I told him anyhow— and right away he said he'd like to come. "Don't worry, Gail. He'll be here."

Gail turns to Kathy and asks, "Do I look all right?"

I'd have just said "Sure," but Kathy brushes an

imaginary piece of lint off Gail's sleeve and does something to the collar of her shirt before she says, "You look fine. Let's talk about something else so you won't feel so nervous."

Obediently, Gail says, "I'm really going to miss the beach this summer. The ocean."

"Mostly, I'm going to miss being busy," Kathy says, "because it's when I'm not busy that I worry most about Matthew."

I can sort of understand what she means, because I get this waiting-for-the-other-shoe-to-drop feeling when I'm not busy. It's really tense around here lately, with scientists still disappearing for days at a time and the ones who stay here working even later than usual. Dad's preoccupied, and Mom's crabbier than ever—especially when Dad's gone.

Jacob comes out of the building and thanks us for waiting, and I can't help noticing that he and Gail manage not to look at each other. When we get to the PX, I see that the *Denver Post* is here already, so I ask Jacob to get me a chocolate sundae while I buy Dad's paper now instead of waiting till later when the cashier's line is a mile long.

When I sit down in front of my sundae, I announce, "Still more of those kamikaze attacks on our ships."

"Those are the suicide bombers, no?" Jacob says as I hand him the paper. He glances at the headlines, then refolds the paper and hands it back to me. "I wish it would not be necessary to invade the Japanese homeland," he says. "My father believes the casualties will be many times those in the battle for Okinawa, and the United States suffered its worst losses in the Pacific there."

Uh-oh. That's the last thing Kathy wants to hear. I glance over at Gail, expecting her to change the subject, but she's looking across the table at Jacob, and she has this sappy expression on her face. I can hardly believe my ears when she says, "My dad read somewhere that ordinary citizens in Japan are going to be given pikes so they can help fight off the invaders."

"What good do they think pikes are going to be against machine guns and grenades?" I ask her, trying to make Kath feel a little better.

Gail shrugs. "Dad says it's part of their culture to never give up. Something to do with honor," she says. "He told me about all these civilians who killed themselves when our troops occupied one of the islands—I think he said it was Saipan. Whole families just waded into the sea and drowned, or else parents threw their children off a cliff and then they jumped off, too."

Beside me, Jacob exclaims, "Then it is true that history repeats itself! The ancient Hebrews did something almost the same at Masada, when they could no longer withstand the Roman soldiers' siege—except at Masada, the men used their swords, first on their loved ones and then on themselves. They robbed the conquerors of their victory by refusing to be defeated and enslaved."

I'm making a mental note to look up Masada, feeling relieved that the conversation has moved away from the war in the Pacific, when Gail says, "I can't imagine men killing their own families like that. I can't even imagine how our soldiers would bring themselves to kill a bunch of women and children carrying pikes, even if they are our enemies." She's looking at Jacob when she says it, but Kathy's the one who answers.

"Enemies or not, my brother could never bring himself to kill women and children. He would never do that."

Jacob turns to her and says, "Your brother is a soldier, Kathy?" He sounds polite and interested.

"Matthew's been overseas for more than a year," she tells him.

"The Matthew you remember would not do that, Kathy, but you must remember that soldiers are trained to kill. And if American forces must invade Japan, once they land, they must either kill or be killed," Jacob says.

Or maybe both, I add silently. Kathy is staring down at her banana split, and since Gail seems to have forgotten that she doesn't like to talk about war news, I figure it's up to me to steer the conversation away from the subject of an invasion. "When you come right down to it, Gail, American servicemen have been killing women and children all along," I tell her. "Think of all the civilian deaths when we firebombed Tokyo. And when the Allies bombed Berlin and Dresden. Most of those civilians had to be women and children, because all but the oldest men are in the army."

Jacob stands up and says, "Please excuse me. I must leave now." He walks across the dance floor, dodging the jitterbugging couples in what looks like an odd dance of his own. I lose sight of him, then see him again as he makes his way through a crowd of GIs standing near the door.

"Why did he leave like that?" Gail demands, breaking the stunned silence. "Was it something I said?"

I shake my head, and feeling about two inches high, I admit, "It was what *I* said. I shouldn't have mentioned bombing Dresden—Jacob was really upset when it was destroyed."

"Oh," Gail says, and after an uncomfortable silence, she turns to Kathy and says, "Let's go home."

I stare after them, wondering how *I* ended up the villain when the whole thing was Gail's fault. Then I watch the last of my ice cream melt, wishing I hadn't agreed to invite Jacob to come with us, wishing I'd kept my big mouth shut about Dresden, hoping Jacob's still my friend. The smooth, white mound of ice cream slumps into a puddle of chocolate sauce, and I pick up Dad's paper and head for the door.

I'm leaving a leather-working class at the youth center on Wednesday when Kathy calls for me to wait up. She admires the wallet I finished today, and I admire the basket she made. She doesn't mention Friday's "celebration," and neither do I.

"Where's Gail?" I ask, wondering if she's still mad at me.

"Babysitting up on Bathtub Row. I'd babysit there for free, if I could have a bubblebath." Kathy sighs and says, "I wish my Dad was important enough to rate a real house with a tub. Can you imagine a town this size with only six bathtubs?"

Mom complains about only having a shower, too, but not half as much as Kathy does. "Hey, look," I say, pointing. "There's something you don't see every day—an ambulance with a police escort." My eyes widen when I see another police car bringing up the rear.

Kathy says, "Maybe you don't see it every day,

but I saw the same thing last week."

"You're kidding."

"It was about this same time of day, too."

Something's definitely going on. "Where do you think they're headed, Kath?"

"Well, if they continue in that direction, they'll come to a whole lot of buildings inside a big fence with barbed wire on top and MPs guarding—"

"Okay, so that was a dumb question. If we take it for granted that they're going to the Lab, the real question is, *why* are they going to the Lab?"

Kathy shrugs. She's a lot better at criticizing my questions than she is at answering them.

"Listen, Kath. There's got to be either something valuable or somebody important in that ambulance, right?"

"Unless it's a decoy. They might want people to think they've got something in the ambulance, but they really put whatever it is in the trunk of one of the police cars."

"Holy cow! That would be really clever, but I'm not sure the military has enough imagination to think of it."

"We could walk past the Lab gate, if you want," Kathy says.

Good old Kathy. "Let's go."

We're within sight of the guard house when we see a police car turn out of the gate, and I hold my breath until I see the ambulance and the other police car turn out behind it.

"So we don't know anything more than we did before," Kathy says.

"Oh, yes, we do. We know that whatever they

brought in is so important they even have to guard it inside the Lab fence." The mysterious procession passes us, headed back the way it came, and I say, "See if you can remember exactly when you saw that little convoy before. We need to see if there's a pattern to when they come, okay?"

"Shh—I'm thinking." We walk a dozen or so steps and she says, "It was a week ago today."

"Are you sure, Kath?"

She gives me one of her looks and says, "Of course I'm sure. I saw them when I was coming back from the commissary, and the last time I went there was to buy the candles for that birthday cake I baked for you."

Bingo! "Now we have to figure out whether they come on a once-a-week schedule or every day."

"Or completely at random. It might have been a coincidence that they came on the same day of the week twice in a row," Kathy says. "We'd better make up a schedule of our own," she adds, sounding almost as excited as I feel. "We have to decide which of us is going to watch each day, and we have to figure out a bunch of different places to watch from."

"I don't get it."

Kathy gives an exaggerated sigh. "Look. If this is as important as you think it is, wouldn't the MPs in those police cars be keeping an eye out for anything suspicious? Like the same two people always waiting at the same place, watching them go by?"

I feel a chill of excitement. "We could stand at a bus stop. Then they wouldn't think a thing about it—especially if it was always at the same time of day."

Kathy says, "I still think we'd better take turns."

"Then I'll watch for them tomorrow," I tell her. "Listen, I'm supposed to meet Jacob, so I'd better go." I head for the PX, hoping I'll be able to keep my mind on ping-pong instead of wondering about that ambulance.

Chapter Twenty-Four

I close Notes on the Secret Project and look across the kitchen table at Kathy. "Okay, Kath, now we know that for three weeks in a row those police cars and the ambulance have made some kind of delivery to the Lab on the same day of the week and at about the same time."

"How come you're so sure they're bringing something in?" Kathy asks. "They might be coming here to get something, you know."

I stare at her. "But what would they be getting? And where would they be taking it?"

Kathy shrugs. "What would they be bringing, and where would they be bringing it from?" When I don't answer, she says, "Look, Fritz, I don't think we're going to find out anything more than we already know."

"Yeah. I guess you're right. But it sure is discouraging to have something like this going on right under our noses and not have any idea what it means."

"It's not like we're the only ones in the dark," Kathy says. "What if you were one of those MPs in the police cars? What if you were driving that ambulance? You don't think *they* know what's going on, do you? Nobody knows, Fritz. Except maybe the scientists with white badges. My dad says most of the people who work at the Lab don't have the slightest idea what's being done there."

"That must be really frustrating. How do they stand it?" I sure couldn't.

"Not everybody's as curious as you are, Fritz."

True. Most people probably wonder about what's going on here the same way they wonder what makes planes stay up. "I'd still like to know what they're bringing in here every week. Or maybe taking out," I add quickly.

Kathy says, "What I'd like to know is, when are our fathers going to finish this project of theirs and end the war so—"

"—so Matthew can come home." I finish the sentence for her and then say, "I guess you don't want to watch for the ambulance anymore, right?"

"Right. I think it's a waste of time. We aren't going to find out anything else."

After Kathy leaves, I sprawl on my bed and read Notes on the Secret Project from cover to cover, just to cheer myself up. So I can see that I really have found out a lot. When I finish, I roll over on my back and stare at the ceiling. I've collected a whole lot of information, but I still don't know much about the project. Heck, I don't really know anything more than I knew the first week we were here—that the scientists are working on some kind of military technology that's supposed to end the war.

Actually, I do know one more thing—the project has something to do with explosives. But everybody knows that from all those rumblings down in the canyons. I get up, and instead of putting the notebook in my knapsack, I put it on the shelf in my closet with all of last year's school papers, underneath the box that has my ice skates in it. The skates that I hardly ever used 'cause I was scared of running into Lonny and Red—or rather, scared they would run into me.

I shut the closet door and then open it again. Security probably wouldn't bother to go through school papers, but just in case, I slip the notebook inside my three-hole binder, sort of in the middle of my compositions. For camouflage.

When I turn around, I see my knapsack leaning against the wall and realize I'm not going to need it now that I won't be carrying Notes on the Secret Project around with me. I'm about to take out the other notebooks and toss the empty knapsack into the back of my closet, but then I realize that it's become such a part of me I'd feel almost naked without it. So I put it on and head for the PX to meet Jacob.

I clatter down the steps, glad that nobody but Kathy knew about the Secret Project notebook. It was pretty stupid to think I could figure out what's going on over at the Lab. Still, it was fun to try, and I'm going to miss adding the stuff I found out—especially the rumors and observations. I'll still add to the other notebooks, of course, but it sure won't be the same.

Jacob easily wins the first two games in spite of my five-point handicap. "I think you have some worry today, Fritz," he says, frowning across the table at me.

"Sort of," I admit.

His frown deepens and he says, "You must concentrate on the game instead of this worry if you are to win." He holds up the ball and asks, "Which do you choose to do, play or worry?"

I hold out my hand, and he tosses me the ball.

Before I serve, I put the Secret Project notebook out of my mind and tell myself to concentrate.

"Now you are a worthy opponent," Jacob says when the score is tied at 20 to 20. I finally beat him, and he seems almost as pleased as I am. I want to play another game, but he refuses. "You must savor your victory," he says, "because tomorrow I take away another point from your handicap."

Jacob waits with me while I buy Dad's paper, so I figure Lonny and Red must have come in. Yup, there they are, hanging around the rack of comic books again. Probably hoping to catch me without my "body-guard." I'm glad Jacob keeps an eye out for them, but I wish he didn't have to. *He* doesn't seem to care that I'm scared of those goons, but it bothers me a lot. I especially hate not being able to ride on the canyon trail by myself for fear they'll be fishing in the stream down at the bottom.

Jacob and I leave the PX together, and I head for home, fretting about Lonny and Red. Oh, well. At least I don't run into them a couple times a day like I did during the school year. They never show up at the youth center, so about the only place our paths cross is at the PX, and I only see them there once or twice a week. Just often enough to keep me on the alert.

Chapter Twenty-Five

I'm eating a late breakfast when somebody knocks on the door. It's Kathy, and this time Gail's with her. "What's up?" I ask. Kathy looks so excited I almost ask her if Matthew's coming home after all, but when she waves a copy of *The Daily Bulletin* at me, I'm glad I didn't.

"Did you see this?" she asks. I shake my head, so she reads it aloud: "'Residents are reminded that no mail may be sent without disclosure of the full name of the sender. If the signature is other than the sender's full name, a slip of paper with the full name written on it may be enclosed in the envelope. This paper will be removed before the letter is mailed. Letters that do not include this identification will be destroyed.'"

I grin and say, "Sounds like a response to Honey Bunch, alias Irate Customer, doesn't it?" This is the first good thing that's happened since I abandoned the Secret Project notebook.

"Wait till you hear the next notice," Gail says. "I think it's an answer to the complaint you got your mom to make."

Kathy starts to read again. "'The public is assured that security measures under no circumstances will delay the sending of mail by more than 48 hours. Any correspondence of a critical nature may be

174

marked with the words *Please Expedite.'*"

Slowly I repeat, "Please expedite. Don't you have anything that needs to be expedited?"

"I'm sure we can think of something," Gail says. "Let's all go over to my place—I told Mom I'd be right back."

Gail's mother waves to us from the balcony where she's having coffee with a neighbor, and we go inside, stepping over the crayons and paper Gail's little brother has strewn on the living room floor.

"Look at this," Kathy says, picking up a drawing of a sad-faced man in a black and white striped shirt, peering from a barred window. "This is exactly how I feel—like I'm a prisoner here on the Hill. And that gives me an idea."

She picks up a red crayon and tears a piece of paper from the kid's tablet. In big letters that go across the top of the paper, she writes H E L P! And underneath, in smaller letters, she prints I AM BEING HELD PRISONER IN A TOP-SECRET SCIENTIFIC LAB IN LOS ALAMOS, NEW MEXICO.

I feel a chill of excitement when I read the forbidden words. It's a good thing Security doesn't put hidden *cameras* in scientists' apartments. I'm about to tell Kathy she'd better chew up that piece of paper and swallow it when I see that Gail's printing PLEASE EXPEDITE! diagonally across the top left corner of an envelope.

Wait a minute—Gail's too sensible to think they can get away with anything like this. And too much of a goody-goody, besides. This must be the girls' way of blowing off steam.

"Should I address the envelope to President

Truman?" Gail asks, looking up.

"The censors will think they're dealing with some kind of crackpot if we send it to the president," Kathy says. "Who should we send it to, Fritz?"

"How about the sheriff?" I suggest, getting into the spirit of their little game, and I watch while Gail prints in block letters,

SHERIFF'S OFFICE
SANTA FE, NEW MEXICO

When she finishes, she looks at it thoughtfully and says, "You know, I'm not sure we should mail this."

I'm a hundred percent certain we shouldn't, but before I can say so, Kathy sort of explodes. "You are such a fraidy cat, Gail! Nothing happened when we mailed all those other fake letters, did it?"

It's not a game after all.

Gail frowns and says, "But this is different—it's addressed to a real person, and what you wrote is supposed to be kept secret. Top secret, like you said. What if it's actually delivered to the sheriff's office? We'd be in big trouble. Trouble with Security. Maybe even trouble with the FBI. What if they think we're traitors?"

I'm looking from one of them to the other, kind of like watching a ping-pong game, when Kathy says, "Honestly, Gail! The censors would never let anything like that get through—they'll know it's a prank, for gosh sake."

"They didn't know the Irate Postal Customer letter was a prank," I remind her. "They answered it, didn't they?"

176

"They answered the complaint your mom made, Fritz," Kathy says with exaggerated patience, and I figure she's probably right. She turns to Gail and says, "We'll let Fritz decide whether to mail it or not, okay?"

Gail nods, looking relieved, and Kathy says, "It's your choice, Fritz. Do you want to have some fun with the censors, or are you going to be a fraidy cat like Gail?"

Great. Why did she have to put it like that? I glance from one of them to the other. Gail's expression says she's counting on me to put a stop to this, but Kathy's got the same determined look she had last fall when she was skunking me at ping-pong. A look that says she's pretty sure I'm not going to measure up, and she isn't going to waste her time on me if I don't.

"Well, Fritz?"

"It's your funeral, Kathy," I tell her. She seems half surprised and half pleased, but Gail's expression shows she can't believe I've let her down like this. I can't believe it, either, so I take the envelope from her and say, "If you're really worried, Gail, I'll see that this gets mailed. That way, nobody will know you had anything to do with it."

She gives me a grateful look, and for about ten seconds I feel like some kind of hero. After that, I feel stupid.

On my way home, I think about tearing up the letter and flushing it—sometime when I'd be flushing anyway, of course, since the drought this summer has made the water shortage here even worse. But right away I realize that destroying the letter would never work. Kathy's going to expect a full report on how I managed to mail it, and she'd know right away if I made up some story to tell her. Chickening out would be even worse than being a fraidy cat.

Since I'm up early anyway so I can find some-body to mail the girls' latest fake letter, I might as well identify some summer plants in the meadow while it's still cool. I'm filling my canteen when Mom pauses at the kitchen door on her way to work and asks, "Where are you off to this morning? Hiking with Jacob again?"

"Not today. I'm going out to identify some plants, among other things."

Mom says goodbye, and when I think she's had enough of a head start I set off for the Lab gate to put my plan into action. I was awake half the night, wor-rying and trying to figure out what to do, and I finally decided to stop one of the Mexican maintenance work-ers and ask him to put the letter in the Tech Area censors' box. It's a perfect solution, 'cause a person who doesn't read English can't very well wonder why some kid would be writing to the sheriff.

I station myself where I can see the people hurry-ing toward the Lab gate but won't attract attention from the MPs. I see a likely looking candidate, but he brushes past me impatiently before I can say any-thing. I walk along with the next guy I pick, but he shakes his head. Finally, I see an older-looking man, and he listens courteously, nodding as I speak. I hand him the letter and start out toward the meadow, glad to have that over with.

I can't imagine a nicer morning—bright and sunny, with a little breeze that carries the scent of pine. It makes me think of the composition Manny wrote last fall, and that makes me glad I've left the ugly, sprawling Tech Area with its barbed wire-topped fence behind me.

I come back from my expedition after a couple hours of walking in the meadow. I only found two new plants and one new species of butterfly, and I didn't see any birds I haven't already identified. But heck, it was a great walk.

I'm almost home when I see a military police car parked in front of our building. I tell myself it's a coincidence, and I keep on walking, 'cause it would look pretty suspicious if I suddenly turned around. But the closer I come to the car, the faster my heart beats. I manage to walk at the same pace anyhow, and I even give the cops who are sitting in it a curious look as I go by, figuring that's what I'd do ordinarily.

I feel a lot better when I've gotten past the car—until I hear the metallic sound of doors slamming. And then one of those guys is in front of me and the other's beside me. My heart's beating so fast now it's like one of those jackhammers workmen use to rip up the pavement.

"You Fritz Madden?"

"Yeah, why?" I show them my pass before they can ask to see it. "That's my real name—Franklin," I explain, but they don't seem to care.

"We have some questions for you, young man."

"What kind of questions?" As if I didn't know. I should have let Kathy think I was a fraidy cat.

One of the MPs shows me an envelope and says, "Questions about this."

"Yeah, what about it?" Dad says if somebody

catches you red-handed, you'd better own up and tell the truth, or from then on, nobody will believe a word you say.

The MPs exchange a quick glance and the older one says, "Have you seen this envelope before?"

"Sure. Somebody asked me to mail it for 'em, so when I went past the Tech Area this morning I gave it to a guy and asked him to put it in the censors' box. Why?" I'm starting to feel more confident now. Must be all the practice I've had dealing with Lonny and Red.

"Can you describe this person for us?"

"Middle-aged, maybe older. Looked Mexican, or maybe Indian. Probably a maintenance worker."

The MP who's doing all the talking says, "Not the person you gave the envelope to outside the Tech Area—the one who gave it to you in the first place."

I'm tempted to describe Lonny but decide I'd better not. "Just an ordinary looking kid. You know, brown hair. Wearing jeans and a polo shirt."

"A kid? Somebody you've seen around school?"

"Sure, but I don't know many of the upperclassmen. What's this all about, anyhow? What's this kid done? What's going on?" Taking the offensive sometimes can make an opponent back off—and I've got to make this cop back off before I have to tell an out-and-out lie.

The MP puts the envelope in the inner pocket of his jacket and says, "Nothing to worry about. And thanks—you've been a big help. A lot of kids would have tried to run off."

"'The wicked flee when no man pursueth, but the innocent are brave as a lion,'" I quote.

"The *righteous*," says the young guy who's just

been standing there—making sure I didn't run off, apparently.

What the heck is he talking about? "Huh?"

"It's the righteous who are brave as a lion, not the innocent." The officer turns toward his partner and says, "I figured this kid wasn't the one we were after, because if he'd been up to something he'd of slipped that envelope into the censors' box we use, down at the Trading Post. And he wouldn't be wearing that knapsack. Boy, talk about being easy to identify!"

But this kid was too dumb to think of that. The MPs get back in their car, and I head toward the apartment, glad they don't know how weak my legs are right now. Great. Here comes Timmy.

"Why were those policemen waiting for you, Fritz? Do they think you did something bad? Are they gonna come back and take you to jail?"

Soon as he stops for a breath, I say, "They wanted me to help them, Timmy. They asked me about a kid from school. Somebody they think might have done something bad. Okay?"

Timmy looks relieved—or maybe disappointed. "Will that kid from school have to go to jail, Fritz?"

"They don't put kids in jail," I tell him, wondering what they do to them instead. Soon as I'm inside our apartment, I take off my knapsack and sort of collapse on the sofa. My heart's racing and my skin suddenly feels cold. Clammy. Some kind of delayed reaction, I guess, but better now than when those guys were talking to me. Interrogating me.

I feel a little better after I've had a glass of water, and I'm about to go up to Kathy's and warn the girls not to send any more fake letters when an awful thought hits me. What if those guys didn't really believe me? What if they're watching, waiting for me to lead them to the person who gave me the letter to mail? *What if I'm under surveillance?*

My legs go weak all over again, and I take a couple of deep breaths to calm myself. How the heck am I going to warn the girls without leading the MPs right to their door? Or rather, doors. Slowly I become conscious of a sound coming up from the apartment below ours. Kind of a continuous *RRRrrrrrrr, RRRrrrrrr.* Timmy playing trucks.

Bingo! I'll have Timmy deliver a message. In my room, I tear a blank page out of my Modern American Indians notebook, and disguising my handwriting, I carefully print: "Do not continue the game you and your friend have been playing. It is too dangerous. Do not come to my place, because that's dangerous, too."

Trouble is, that won't stop Kathy. She'll be on her way here to say, "Tell me, Fritz," the minute she reads this. I'll have to come up with a plan.

"Meet me at the place we went the day school got out. Be there half an hour after you receive this note. Write YES on the bottom of the note and return it to me immediately so I'll know you're coming." In a flash of inspiration, I go back and make little hearts to dot every "i" the way "Honey Bunch" did.

I fold the paper and tape around all the edges, seal it into an envelope, go over to the heating register and call, "Hey, Timmy."

The motor noises downstairs stop. "Hi, Fritz. Want to play trucks?"

"How would you like to earn a dime, instead?"

"I'll be right up!"

"Hey, wait! Ask your mom if you can run an errand for me, okay?"

About half a minute later he's back. "She said I can do it. And she hopes it's a long errand, 'cause she could use a little peace and quiet."

"Okay, Timmy. Come on upstairs and I'll tell you what to do." By the time I get to the door, he's already peering through the screen. I show him the envelope and say, "All you have to do is take this up to Kathy's house, wait while she reads it, and bring me back an answer. Okay?"

"Okay," Timmy says, reaching for the envelope. "I like Kathy. She lives right upstairs from my friend Eric."

"You can't stay and play with Eric, and you can't give the envelope to anybody but Kathy," I say as I hand it to him. "Understand?" He nods, but just to make sure, I tell him, "You have to come straight back with Kathy's answer. Got that?"

Timmy nods, and then he whispers, "It's a love letter, right?"

"Wrong. Now go on."

I stand by the window, watching for police cars or anything else that seems suspicious. I figure even if they've got me staked out, they probably aren't close enough to see Timmy coming up and down our balcony steps. At least I hope they aren't.

There's Timmy now, galloping along the way little kids do. It looks like he's kept his part of the bargain, so I fish in my pocket and bring out two nickels.

"I've got your answer," he says when I meet him on the balcony.

"Good. I've got your money."

Timmy starts to hand me the envelope, then holds it behind him. "That's not a dime. You said a dime."

I empty my pockets, and fortunately I find one. "Okay?" I ask, showing him the coin. He nods, and we make our trade. The envelope has been sealed with *adhesive* tape, but I tear it open and see YES written in huge letters under my note.

So far so good. I head for the PX, planning to look at the comic books while I wait for the girls so it won't be so obvious that I've come to meet somebody. I'm almost there when I see a police car coming toward me. I hold my breath, waiting for it to go by, but it stops and the driver rolls down the window. My heart sinks when I see it's one of those same two guys. The younger one. *Now* what?

"Hey, Fritz!" he calls. He beckons to me, and I force myself to cross the road. "Hop in back," he says, "or up front, if you'd rather. We need you to look at some pictures."

"Mug shots, you mean?" I ask.

"Here, we call 'em pass photos. Get in—you're going to help us find that kid who gave you the envelope."

Great. I walk around and climb in the front seat, just on general principles, and then I see Gail and Kathy on their way to meet me at the PX. Kathy looks straight ahead, but Gail points to the car and then claps her hands over her mouth.

The driver laughs. "Anybody you know?" he asks.

Making my voice sound really disgusted, I say, "Yeah. They're in my class, and now they'll tell everybody in town that I was picked up by the police."

"Your neighbors already know we were questioning you," the driver says cheerfully. "We attracted a lot of attention while we were waiting for you to show up."

"Yeah, I know." I sure hope Timmy spreads that story I told him so nobody asks Mom what was going on.

The car pulls up at the headquarters building, and we go inside. The older officer gets up from a desk and takes me down a hall and into a room with a long table covered with photos laid out in alphabetical order.

"Good grief!" I say. "All those?"

"All the boys in grades nine through twelve," the officer says, and as he sits down opposite me I realize that he's going to be watching my reaction to the pictures. Apparently the younger guy does the socializing and this one does the interrogating.

I lean over the table and slowly move my eyes along the rows of photos, hoping I don't end up getting some completely innocent kid in trouble. Hey, there's Jacob, but it's not a very good picture of him. Finally I shake my head and say, "It wasn't any of these guys."

"You sure about that?"

I nod, and the MP reaches out to pick up one of the photos. Jacob's photo. I must have looked at it a little longer than the others. The officer glances at it and then turns it around to face me. "What about this one?" he asks, and I shake my head.

"Friend of yours?"

"Yeah. We play ping-pong together and stuff like that. Go on hikes."

The officer looks at me for a long time, and I start

to feel uneasy. Finally he says, "Maybe after your last ping-pong game this friend of yours gave you a letter to mail. Maybe you're covering for him."

"Jacob wouldn't do anything I'd have to cover him for. He's the kind of kid who plays chess and listens to Mozart symphonies and always dresses like he's on his way to church or something."

"The kind of kid who doesn't wear jeans and polo shirts."

I nod, hoping this cop doesn't really think it was Jacob. Hoping he doesn't think I was trying to throw them off the track by saying the kid who gave me the letter was wearing jeans. "It definitely wasn't Jacob who gave me the letter to mail," I tell him.

"Then who was it?"

The words come at me like gunfire, and I can't help flinching. "I already told you it wasn't anybody here," I say, and when he narrows his eyes at me, I quickly add, "I'm not answering any more of your questions unless my dad's here."

"Your dad some kind of lawyer?" the officer asks.

"He's a scientist at the Lab."

The MP leans back and says, "That was supposed to be a joke, Fritz. We know who your father is. We know everything there is to know about everybody here on the Hill, and don't you forget it." He sweeps the photos into a pile and then neatens them into a stack. So much for alphabetical order.

"Can I go now?"

The officer nods, and as I leave the room, I can feel his eyes on my back. In the parking lot outside, the younger officer is leaning against his car, talking to a couple of GIs, and he waves to me.

"Hey, Fritz. Were you able to help us any?"

I wave back and say, "Afraid not. Sorry." And then it hits me: The two of them work as a team, one acting mean and the other pretending to be my friend, like in those thrillers I read, and this guy's the friendly one. Well, he doesn't fool me. At least not anymore.

I head for the PX, figuring that even if Security has put me under surveillance, it should be okay for me to go over there and talk to Kathy and Gail. After all, (1) that's where I was headed when the friendly MP picked me up, and (2) he knows the girls saw me in the police car, so it would seem natural enough if they wanted to find out what was going on.

They wave to me from one of the tables, and the minute I join them, Kathy says, "Tell us, Fritz," just like I knew she would.

So I tell them. And when I'm finished, I add, "In case they're watching, expecting me to lead them to the culprit, we probably ought to avoid each other for a couple of days."

They both nod, and Gail says, "You were really clever, Fritz. Clever, and brave, too."

Brave? *Me?* "Well, clever anyhow." And maybe a little bit brave, but mostly very careful about what I said.

"Thanks for not giving us away," Kathy says. It's pretty much the nicest thing she's ever said to me. Actually, it's probably the only nice thing. She's always stood by me, though, and I guess that's more important.

I'm about to leave when Jacob comes over and says, "The two soldiers at the ping-pong table have asked us to join them for a game of doubles, Fritz.

Do you think the girls will excuse you?"

"Sure. I'll be right there." After he leaves, I see that Gail's face has turned that rosy pink again and Kathy looks indignant. "What's the matter?" I ask her.

"He called us 'the girls,' like he didn't know our names," and he asked *you* whether *we* would mind."

"Come on, Kath. He's probably still embarrassed about walking off like that on the last day of school."

Gail gives me a pleading look and says, "Try to get him to come back here with you after the game, okay?"

I glance at Kathy, and she says, "Tell 'the boy' that Gail invited him."

Jacob and I win our first game against the GIs, and when we're changing sides of the table for the next game, I see that Kathy and Gail have turned their chairs so they can watch us play. *Kathy saw me play ping-pong—and win.*

Jacob and I win the second game, too, and after we turn the paddles over to a couple of soldiers who were watching, I say, "Gail and Kathy said for me to bring you back with me after our game. Come on." I walk toward the table and don't let myself glance back to see if he's coming. But from the look on Gail's face, I know he is.

We're sitting there talking when the mean MP stops at our table and lays a heavy hand on my shoulder. "Introduce me to your friends, Fritz," he says.

I swallow hard and say, "Um, these are Gail and Kathy, and that's Jacob."

He looks them over for a few seconds and then he says, "Gail Seely, Kathy Barton, and Jacob Schwartz. Right?"

They're all staring at him with their mouths hanging open, so I say, "Right. I've never been much good with introductions. Sorry." I remind myself that a little while ago he was looking at Jacob's photo, and that his partner probably picked out the girls' photos after he saw them coming down the sidewalk. Cops are trained to be observant, after all.

I glance at Jacob and see that he's even paler than he was the day we heard that Hitler had killed himself. *But this time, Jacob better not leave.* I glance at the MP and see that he's watching Jacob, giving him one of those long looks like he gave me a little while ago, and I've got an awful feeling about what's going to happen next.

The MP says, "Tell your friends good-bye, Jacob Schwartz. I'm taking you back to headquarters for questioning." Jacob doesn't move, and he goes even paler. The cop snarls, "What's the matter, don't you understand English?"

"What I do not understand is why I must go with the police," Jacob says in a tight voice. "I have done nothing wrong." He's gripping the edge of the table so hard his knuckles are white.

"We'll decide that after we've questioned you. Now get up!"

Kathy says, "Wait a minute. What are you going to question him about?"

The MP looks down at her and says, "About why he asked his friend Fritz, here, to mail a certain letter for him, not that it's any business of yours."

Now Kathy goes pale. "That wasn't Jacob. It was me."

"Nice try, Kathy, but I don't believe you," the cop says.

Kathy meets his eyes and recites, "Help! I'm being held prisoner in a top-secret laboratory in Los Alamos, New Mexico."

Looking smug now, the cop sits down and says, "Now we're getting somewhere." He pulls his chair up to the table and asks sternly, "What did you think you were doing, writing something like that?" His face is about three inches from Kathy's.

"It was a joke," she whispers. "I knew the censors wouldn't—"

"This isn't a joking matter, miss," he interrupts. "Not only have you distracted Security personnel from our work of protecting the scientists and the secrecy of this project, you've caused a lot of unpleasantness for your friends, too."

Kathy begins to sniffle, and I stare down at the table. I hear Jacob say, "Excuse me, officer, but am I free to leave?"

The cop waves him away, and I watch Jacob head for the door while I listen to Kathy being chewed out. Did this guy really think Jacob gave me the envelope to mail, or was he using Jacob to force a confession out of one of the girls? Maybe he figured writing a note like that was more the kind of thing a girl would do. And he somehow knew that being bawled out at the PX with everybody watching and listening would be a worse punishment for Kathy than being taken back to headquarters.

When the MP finally finishes with her, he sits there for a minute and watches her cry. And then he says, "No more letters. You understand?" Kathy nods, and he turns to me and says, "And no more lies, not even for your girlfriend. You hear?"

I'm about to tell him she's just a *friend* friend, but I think better of it. Instead I say, "I didn't lie. I told you 'a kid' gave me the letter, and you assumed it was a boy. And after I looked at the photos, I said 'It wasn't any of these guys,' and that was the honest truth."

The man's eyebrows draw together in a frown, and I realize I should have kept my big mouth shut. "I *have* to tell the truth," I say, trying to talk my way out of my mistake, "because I'm such a terrible liar. Meaning that I don't lie very well."

"I'll have to remember that, Fritz," the MP says, making it sound like a threat. He gives us each another long look—even Gail—and then he leaves. One of the GIs puts a nickel in the juke box, and the music pours out, breaking the silence that had fallen over the nearby tables.

The three of us sit there without saying anything while Kathy pulls herself together. After she's wiped her eyes and blown her nose she takes a deep breath and says, "I guess you were right, Gail. We shouldn't have mailed it."

"But you were right that the censors wouldn't let it get through," Gail says. Lowering her voice, she asks, "Do you think Security's going to say anything about this to your parents?"

"I sure hope not," Kathy says, looking like she's about to cry again.

"Don't worry, Kath," I tell her. "Nobody's going to do anything that would distract the scientists from their work." Didn't that mean MP lay off me once he knew I wasn't going to answer any more questions without Dad there?

191

Kathy wipes her eyes again and says, "Look, Fritz—the ping-pong table's free. Let's play."

"I don't play triples, Kath. Just singles and doubles."

Kathy goes *tsk!* and then she says, "Gail's going to watch. Come on."

"I like the way you take it for granted that I'm going to play," I tell her. Boy, she must have really been impressed when she watched that doubles game a little while ago.

"What's the matter, Fritz? Afraid I'll skunk you again?"

Gail says, "You shouldn't talk to him like that, Kathy."

"Yeah," I say as I get up. "You shouldn't talk to me like that."

I follow Kathy across the empty dance floor toward the ping-pong table, hoping that a couple of games will help me forget what happened today. And hoping that I can beat Kathy at least once.

Chapter Twenty-Six

It's true. There's nothing like an early morning ride on the mesa. The sky has a rosy glow, the mountains in the distance loom up purple, and the only sound is birds twittering. But give it a couple of hours, and the glare and the dust will wipe out all the color. Plus you won't be able to hear yourself think for the trucks and the construction noise. It's hard to believe that they're still doing construction. More lab buildings, more apartments, more—

"A day like this is worth getting up for, right?" Manny says, turning in the saddle to look back at me. I nod, and he says, "I'm taking you someplace me and my grandpa used to go. Haven't been there for a couple of years now."

"You sure you remember how to get there?" I ask. He gives me this really disgusted look as he turns away, and I remind myself that he hasn't gotten us lost yet.

We leave the road and follow a narrow trail that snakes across a slope, and I'm having a great time till we turn into a gully that sort of plunges downhill. I grab the pommel of the saddle and hang on, not caring one bit that "only an amateur" would be caught dead doing that.

We've been making our way almost straight down for what seems like forever when Manny stops and says, "What the—" He lets loose a string of Spanish that's got to be cuss words. Brownie pins back her ears, and I pat her shoulder and tell her everything's fine, even though it obviously isn't.

When Manny's through cussing, he looks back at me and says, "Come on up here and see what them gringos has done."

I urge Brownie forward and come out next to Manny on a *road.* A one-lane dirt road covered with tire tracks. "How the heck did this get way back in here?"

Instead of answering, Manny says, "Come on. We're gonna see where it goes to."

We ride along side by side for a while, and I'm wondering what we'd do if we heard some kind of vehicle coming when I see a fence across the road up ahead. It's another of those chainlink fences with barbed wire strung around the top. We're too far away to read the sign on it, but I'm pretty sure it's one of those official government signs that say DANGER! KEEP OUT! in both English and Spanish.

"Come on," Manny says.

"But the sign—"

"It says 'Keep Out,' Fritz. It don't say you can't look."

My skin prickles like all those little hairs are standing on end, and the closer we come to that fence the pricklier I get. "Some kind of buildings," I whisper. "And a water tower, too."

A shot rings out and a voice yells "Halt!" *Not a water tower—a guard house!*

I'm paralyzed with fear, but Brownie's not. Before I know what's happening, she's thundering down the road behind Coal Dust, and I'm hanging on for dear life. Sirens wail, and Brownie lays back her ears again.

Ahead of us, Manny and Coal Dust turn into the gully, and Brownie puts on a little spurt of speed to catch up with them. Now it's so steep and rough underfoot that we can't make very good time, but at least nobody can see us from the road. We haven't gone very far when I hear the hum of a motor. My mouth goes dry. *MPs! They'll see our tracks.*

I hear the crunch of tires and hold my breath as the sound gets louder and louder. When it starts to fade away, I realize the car has passed the mouth of the gully, and I start to breathe again. Brownie's so close behind Coal Dust that his tail swishes across her face, and I figure we both wish Manny would ride faster. I try to estimate how far we've come from the road, wonder if it's possible for men on foot to catch up to us.

Uh-oh. I can hear the car coming back, a lot slower now, like maybe those MPs are looking for the place where the hoofprints of two galloping horses leave the road. My heartbeat thuds inside my head, and my mouth is dry as sawdust.

The hum of the motor stops. I hear the slam of a car door—and then another. *They've gotten out!* The crackle of a walkie-talkie fills the air, and we pick up our speed. The branches of cottonwood saplings brush against us, and I'm glad for their shelter.

Finally, Manny reins in Coal Dust, and Brownie crowds up against them. In the distance, I hear the sound of a car and realize that the sirens have stopped. Manny gives me a crooked grin and says, "They've left. You by any chance got a canteen in that knapsack of yours?"

We take turns drinking until the water's gone,

and I ask, "Why didn't they come after us? They know we're up here."

"Probably figured we couldn't be too dangerous, being as we weren't exactly sneaking around. Besides, a patrol car passed us when we was riding along the road right after we left the stable. Once they saw our tracks leading up the gully and got on their walkie-talkies, they probably put two and two together."

I stare at Manny. "You mean they know it was us?"

"They know it was kids. Come on."

"Wait a minute," I say. "What if they're patrolling the road up there and they stop us on our way back to the stable?"

"Before they can start in on us, I'll say, 'Boy, are we glad to see you! We ran into some maniac with a gun down in the canyon.'"

My skin starts to prickle again and I say, "It's hard to believe that guard actually shot at us."

"He fired into the air, Fritz. That was a warning shot."

"What makes you so sure?"

Manny gives me a level look. "'Cause if he'd shot at us, either you or me would be laying back there, dead. I've watched them MPs doing target practice, and they don't miss."

My mouth goes even drier than it was before I had the water, and I wonder if soldiers ever get used to being shot at. "Let's go," I say, and without a word, Manny starts off again.

After a while I say, "Seems like it's taking an awfully long time to get back. You haven't gotten us lost, have you?"

Manny turns around and glares at me. "We're

going back a different way, that's all."

At first I think he's just not owning up to being lost, but then it hits me. We're going back a different way in case the MPs are waiting at the top of the gully. With a good contour map, they could figure out more or less where it starts and just wait for us there instead of chasing us. I grin, wondering how long those cops are going to hang around waiting for us to show up.

It seems like hours before we come into a clearing with a tumble-down shed on the far side and Manny says, "Okay, this is what we're gonna do. I'm leaving Coal Dust here, and we'll both ride back on Brownie. Later on, I'll bring Rosa—she's my cousin— over here, and she'll ride Coal Dust back to the stable. Them MPs won't be looking for two kids riding bareback, or for a girl, either."

Bareback! "I thought you said they wouldn't—"

"That was before I heard that little airplane of theirs flying low along the road," Manny says, interrupting. "Now get that saddle off her."

I'm doing that, remembering that I'd heard the plane but didn't think anything of it, when Manny comes out of the shed with a dented bucket. He works the handle of a nearby pump until a thin stream of water flows from it. While the horses drink, he pumps water into my hands, and after I've drunk enough I pump some for him. Then we take turns pumping water on each other's heads. The cold shock of it takes my breath away, but afterward I'm surprised at how much better I feel.

I'm about to fill my canteen when Manny says, "You'll have to leave that in the shed. Your knapsack,

197

too. I'll get 'em later."

"I can't leave my knapsack here!"

Manny's eyes narrow. "You don't have no choice, Fritz. Take it off."

Reluctantly, I do as he says. "If anybody finds this, they'll know it's mine," I tell him, remembering what that MP said about it making me easy to identify.

"Nobody's gonna find it," Manny says. I follow him into the shed and watch him put it under the saddle and cover it all with a couple of old burlap sacks.

But what if they *do* find it? What's that mean MP going to think if I'm picked up for snooping around a secret area? What's the friendly one going to think when he finds out I ran away when the guard yelled for us to halt? *The wicked flee when no man pursueth, but the righteous are brave as a lion.* That's what he's going to think.

"You ain't getting scared on me now, are you?" Manny asks. I shake my head and follow him over to where Brownie's nibbling on some weeds. It takes a few tries to get both of us on her back, but we manage, and pretty soon a faint path brings us out on the road.

We haven't gone far when we see a jeep coming toward us. "You better let me handle this," Manny says when it slows to a stop beside us. I don't argue with him, 'cause I've never seen four meaner-looking MPs.

"You kids seen anybody else riding along here?" one of them asks, squinting up at us.

Behind me, Manny says, "No comprendo."

One of the guys in the back seat says, "You're wasting your time with the likes of them. Let's go."

They roar off in a cloud of dust, and I ask, "What do you think they'd do if they caught us?"

"They ain't gonna catch us," Manny says, but he doesn't sound as confident as he did earlier.

We ride the rest of the way to the stable without talking, and I concentrate on keeping my mind blank so I don't worry. When Manny slides off Brownie to open the gate of the corral, my mind fills up with one thought: We made it!

But then I see the MP talking to Carlos, one of the stablehands. The officer sees us at the same time, and as he heads toward us, I've got a feeling that it's all over.

"Hey, did you kids happen to see any other riders when you were out?" he asks.

Manny shrugs and starts in with his "No comprendo," but the MP just switches to his idea of Spanish, which doesn't sound anything like what people speak around here. While he and Manny talk, I escape by leading Brownie to the water trough.

I'm hanging up her bridle in the tack room when Carlos, the stablehand comes in. "Where's Coal Dust?" he demands. "And what the heck kind of trouble have you two got yourselves into? That cop out there was full of questions, but I told him I was new here and didn't know nothin'."

"Coal Dust is fine. Manny's going to bring him back later, and Brownie's saddle, too. Listen, I'd better get on out there," I say, picking up a currycomb.

I'm walking toward Brownie when I hear the officer's car start. Manny comes over, looking smug. "We ain't got a thing to worry about," he says.

"Good," I say, glancing up when I hear the drone

of a small plane overhead. "Did you know Carlos covered for us?"

"He's my cousin," Manny says, "but any of 'em would of."

"How come?"

Manny says, "'Cause we gotta stick together. Didn't you hear what that MP in the jeep said—something about 'the likes of them'? They look down on us, Fritz. They ain't necessarily gonna treat us the same as they would you." He turns away, saying, "I got to go find Rosa so she can ride Coal Dust back here for me."

"What about my knapsack?"

"I'll hang it in the tack room, and you can get it tomorrow morning. Go on home and establish yourself an alibi or something. Carlos can groom Brownie." The stablehand reaches for the currycomb, and as I leave, Manny says, "Hey, Carlos, I need to borrow your bicycle."

It's not till I'm back at the apartment that it hits me how tired I am. I pour a big glass of iced tea and head for the sofa, kicking off my shoes so I can put my feet up on the coffee table. I think about getting my Secret Project notebook out of the closet and writing down everything that happened today under Rumors and Observations, but then I think again and decide not to.

Why bother? Everybody knows the Tech Area has expanded into a lot of the canyons around here—we've been hearing the explosions the scientists set off down there long enough. And it makes sense that they'd have fences and guards down there. And that they'd be in contact with the MPs who keep watch on

this whole area. And that they'd want to find anybody who was messing around a restricted site.
Manny and I were lucky they didn't catch us.

The idea of being picked up by the MPs again
gives me the same prickly feeling I get on the back of
my neck every time I think about the guard shooting
at us. Or firing into the air, if Manny's right. I wonder
what the scientists are doing back in that canyon,
anyhow, and why they can't do it in the main Tech
Area. Must be something really dangerous. My neck
starts to prickle even more.

I'm about to go refill my glass when I hear heavy
footsteps on the steps outside and then a sharp knock
at the door. A voice calls, "Military police. Open up—
we know you're in there, Franklin."

My heart sinks, but I manage to call, "Coming!" I
go to the door, still holding my empty glass. "Hey!
What's going on?" I ask, backing up as they open the
screen and come inside.

"That's what we want you to tell us," one of the
officers says. "You can start with explaining how this
happened to be under a couple of burlap sacks in an
old shed outside of town." He holds out my knapsack, but when I reach for it, he says, "Not so fast,
there. We need some answers from you first."

My mind races, trying to think up a believable
story. "There were these two kids," I tell them. "Older
kids—I've seen them around school, but I don't know
their names—and they grabbed my knapsack the
other day and ran off with it. They must of—"

"You're lying," the other MP says. "You were wearing it when I saw you headed toward the stable this
morning. Get your shoes on. We're taking you in to

201

headquarters for questioning."

Next thing I know, they're marching me down the stairs. I'm climbing into the back seat of their car when Timmy hollers, "Mom! Mom! This time they really *are* taking Fritz to jail!" Great. And this time, somebody's sure to ask Mom what's going on. It's a good thing Dad's away again.

At headquarters, I have to hand over my pass, and while the WAC at the desk is copying the information from it, a door opens and an officer brings Manny out. His eyes widen when he sees me. "I never gave 'em your name, Fritz," he says. "Honest!"

"I know you didn't."

"But I had to tell 'em everything else before they'd let Rosa go."

"That's enough, kid," growls the officer. "You sit over there till we see if your buddy, here, tells the same story you did." He gestures to the room Manny came out of, and I go on inside, trying not to think about the interrogations in some of those spy thrillers I've read.

It's just an ordinary office. Not an interrogation room. And it's some grey-haired officer behind the desk instead of that mean cop. He and his partner must be off today, so at least that business about the envelope isn't going to be held against me.

The officer doesn't look up, so I stand in front of his desk, listening to my heartbeat and trying to breathe. Pretty soon a WAC secretary comes in and hands the guy a file folder, and he glances through the papers in it before he finally looks up at me. I look back at him, wondering why he doesn't say something, feeling the sweat soaking my shirt.

Finally, he picks up the top sheet of paper from the file and reads it aloud. "'Franklin Madden, known as Fritz. Age thirteen. Son of Verne Madden, physicist, top secret clearance (presently off-site) and Mona Madden, employed as a secretary at the Lab. Often seen writing in notebooks, which he carries in a knapsack he wears at all times.'"

They've got a file on me!

The officer keeps on reading. "'Questioned on 6 July 1945 in reference to potential security breach found upon investigation to be an adolescent prank. Subject did not admit responsibility, but investigation found him and at least one other young person to be involved. (See attached report.) The aforementioned notebooks contain information about local plant and animal life, Indians, and current events.'"

What if the Secret Project notebook had been in my knapsack with the others?

The officer picks up the next sheet and reads, "'Franklin Madden, known as Fritz, etc. etc. etc. Had in his possession and attempted to mail—"

By now, I'm prickly all over. I stand here, staring at the officer and letting the words wash over me. I can hear him, but it's like he's reading some foreign language. He picks up the third sheet of paper, and I catch the phrase "restricted area."

Finally he closes the file folder and moves it to the corner of his desk. I feel his eyes on me and wish he'd say something.

Finally, he does. "Look at me, Franklin." I do, thankful that my brain seems to be working again. He says, "Somebody has penciled a note here that says 'This kid's too smart for his own good.' Is that true?"

I shrug, and he says, "Well, you're smart enough to realize that you're in serious trouble, aren't you?"

I nod, and he looks at me for a while longer. That's an old trick—he's trying to make me crack. My eyes start to burn, but I manage not to look away.

At last the officer sighs and says. "All right, Franklin. Tell me the whole story, and make sure you don't leave anything out."

I swallow hard and do as I'm told. When I'm through, he looks past me and says, "Send the other kid back in here," and I realize an officer has been standing by the door this whole time. As a witness, or to keep me from running off?

Manny comes in and stands next to me, and the man behind the desk glares at us for a long time before he starts in on his lecture. I'm starting to wonder if he's ever going to stop talking and let us go when finally he says, "You boys better watch your P's and Q's and stay out of places where you don't belong. You've seen what my men can do, and you'd better believe that they'll be watching you from now on. Understand?"

We both nod, and he says, "Go on then, and stay out of trouble. I don't want to see either of you in here again."

Soon as we're out of the building, I ask, "Did they follow you and Rosa when you went back to the clearing?"

Many shakes his head. "They was waiting for us when we got there. Waiting inside the shed. I figure they must of spotted Coal Dust when they flew over in that plane of theirs."

I can't resist saying, "And you thought they weren't

going to bother with us 'cause they knew we were kids."

Manny crams his hands deeper in his pockets. "Used us to practice on, that's what they done. Probably the most excitement any of 'em had since they got here. A nice change from sentry duty and writing traffic tickets for a bunch of eggheads."

"Eggheads?"

"That's what everybody calls all them scientists." Manny gets a funny look on his face, like he just remembered that my father's one of the eggheads.

So he'll know I'm not sore, I say, "Come on. I'll buy us a couple of cokes at the PX."

"How 'bout instead you hoof it back to that old shed with me so's we can get everything back to the stable. You can ride the bike I got from Carlos, and I'll ride Coal Dust and carry Brownie's saddle."

"Sure," I agree, even though that's the last thing I want to do. Manny's not complaining, and he's got to be even more tired than I am. After all, he had to bicycle from the stable to wherever Rosa lives and then ride double all the way back to the shed.

We're trudging along the road when a wreck of a pick-up truck screeches to a stop beside us. It's a couple of the older Spanish-American kids, and Manny's face lights up when he sees them. There's a rapid exchange of questions and answers, and then Manny switches back to English long enough to say, "Pedro's gonna drive me out there. We can toss the bike and Brownie's saddle in the pick-up so he can take 'em to the stable while I ride Coal Dust back."

Manny squeezes into the cab of the pick-up, and I watch it drive off in a cloud of dust. Then I turn around and head toward home.

Chapter Twenty-Seven

"Fritz? *Fritz!*"

I wake with a start and struggle to sit up. "What's wrong? Is it a fire?"

"Shh! Nothing's wrong," Mom whispers, flicking on my light. "Just get dressed, and be quick about it. Wear a heavy sweater. Your jacket's on the chair by the door—you can pick it up on our way out."

My eyes turn to the alarm clock on my desk. We're going out at three in the morning?

"If you're not ready in two minutes, I'm leaving without you," Mom says over her shoulder.

Two minutes! I pull a pair of jeans and a flannel shirt on over my pajamas and rummage in the drawer for a sweater. I'm putting on my socks when Mom comes back to check on me, pointedly looking at the clock. She's got an armful of blankets.

"You can put your shoes on in the car," she says, "assuming you can find them."

I dig one sneaker out from under the bed, the other from behind the waste basket, and follow Mom down the hall with a couple of seconds to spare. At the door, she gestures to my jacket and the picnic basket, pantomimes *Shh!* and heads out into the darkness.

Good grief! We're going on a *picnic?* As Mom and I tiptoe across the balcony and down the steps, something heavy rolls around on the bottom of the basket. What the heck—? Must be the thermos. I stop at the bottom of the stairs to jam my feet into my shoes, hurry along the gravel walk with the laces flapping, and catch up to Mom as she opens the car door.

She shushes me again and gestures to the back seat, so I climb in with the basket, and Mom piles her stack of blankets on my lap—which actually feels pretty good. It's hard to believe the desert gets this cold in mid-July, even at our elevation. I tuck one blanket around my legs, sort of drape another around me, and wonder who's going to be sitting up front.

We head west on the main road, but pretty soon Mom coasts to a stop. Our headlights cut through the darkness and pick up two bulky shapes moving toward us—Kathy and her mother! Both of them are carrying blankets, and Kath has a jug, too.

Mrs. Barton gets in the passenger seat, and I move the picnic basket over to make room for Kathy. "I thought you were supposed to be under house arrest," she says as she gets in.

"Huh?"

"Timmy's been telling everybody that instead of going to jail you have to stay in your room for a month because you and your friend 'did something bad.'"

Great. "Mom made me stay in the apartment for three days, and today—or rather, yesterday—was the last one," I tell her, "and Manny and I didn't do anything bad."

"Just something incredibly stupid," Mom says from the front seat.

"Now, Mona," Mrs. B. says. "Remember, boys will be boys."

Before Mom can say anything to that, Kathy asks, "Where are we going, anyway? I feel like I'm being kidnapped."

I feel like I'm setting out on some kind of adventure.

"You'll know when we get there," Mom says at exactly the same time Kathy's mother says, "We're going to Sawyer's Hill."

Kathy goes *tsk.* "I can't believe you woke me up in the middle of the night for a picnic at the ski slope."

What a grouch. "Come on, Kath. It might be fun. Maybe we'll see some falling stars, or something."

She pulls a blanket up under her chin and says, "In case you didn't notice, Fritz, the sky is completely overcast tonight. Besides, the next really good meteor shower isn't for a couple of weeks yet. It's the Perseids. I sure hope my dad's home then, 'cause we always watch for them."

"Hey, I never knew you were interested in astronomy," I say, wishing I'd said meteor shower instead of falling stars.

"A person can be interested in something without carrying around a notebook on it, you know. I have a sky chart that I study so I can identify the constellations, and Mom got me a book so I could learn the myths and legends about how they were named."

I can tell by Kathy's voice that she's pretty enthusiastic about all that, so how come she never even mentioned it before? Probably for the same reason I don't talk about the Latin names of plants and butterflies.

Kathy leans forward and whispers, "Don't look now, but I think we're being followed."

I do look now, and there's nothing but pitch-black darkness. But as Mom takes the next curve, I can see a faint glow on the road behind us. It's true, then—we aren't the only ones driving up this mountain. Who else would be going to Sawyer's Hill in the wee hours of the morning? And why?

I hear a couple of clicks that tell me Kathy's locking the doors on her side of the car, and suddenly that seems like a good idea, so I lock the ones on this side. Mom doesn't say anything, and I notice that she's leaning forward, like she's trying to see a little farther ahead in the darkness.

"Are they still behind us?" Kathy whispers.

Being as there's no place to turn around on this narrow, winding road, I figure they have to be, but when I look, everything's solid black. No, there they are. Must have just come around a curve, 'cause now I can see two small, pale circles of light inching along back there.

Mom shifts into a lower gear as the car toils up a long, straight stretch, but the distance between us and those headlights seems to stay the same.

"You don't think they're going to try to force us off the road, do you?" Kathy whispers.

I hadn't even considered the possibility. Till now. "Why would they want to do that?" I ask her, remembering that there aren't any guard rails.

"Why would they want to follow us in the first place? Why would they be coming up here, Fritz?"

"Maybe for the same reason we are—whatever that is."

We lose sight of them as Mom creeps around the next curve, and Kathy whispers, "What if they're coming up here *because* we are?"

"Yeah," I whisper back, remembering the hilarious story our English class wrote, with each person adding a sentence. "Maybe they're from Security, and they want to make sure we're not planning to meet some spy and give away secret information."

"Or," Kathy says, "maybe it's the spy driving that car, and maybe he thinks we're his contacts, and when he finds out we're not, he'll have to kill us to keep from blowing his cover."

"Except that it doesn't work that way," I tell her. "Any spy worth his salt would get himself up there way ahead of time so he could make sure—"

Kathy goes *tsk* again and says, "Come on, Fritz. It's just a story. This is fiction, for gosh sake."

"It should be accurate anyway, Kath. True-to-life."

The car rolls to a stop and Mom says, "Well, here we are." Before she turns off the headlights I see a row of parked cars. What the heck is going on up here?

"Looks like we aren't the only ones who thought of this," Mrs. B. says.

"At least there's plenty of room," Mom says.

We all pile out of the car, and while we're gathering up the blankets and picnic stuff, I hear the sound of a straining engine.

"Come on, let's go," Kathy says, and I wonder if she half believed that story we were making up.

The other car pulls into the parking area, and the beam of its headlights throws our shadows ahead of us, tall as giants. Then it's dark again, except for the pale glow of the flashlights Mom and Mrs. B. brought to light our way. Seconds later, I hear car doors slam, exactly like they did the day those cops were waiting for me in front of the apartment. I can't help walking faster, but I slow down again when I hear women's laughter instead of a deep voice shouting *Halt!*

"Not military police, apparently," Kathy whispers.

"Probably not spies, either."

Our mothers choose a spot a little distance from anyone else. We spread out a couple of blankets to sit on and then each of us wraps up in another blanket.

"Look, I'm a mummy," I say, lying flat on my back.

"You're a dope, Fritz," Kathy says, but she doesn't sound like she means it.

I hear the click of the flashlight and see Mrs. B. checking her watch. "Three forty-five, Mona," she says quietly. "Only fifteen more minutes."

"Fifteen more minutes till what?" I ask, sitting up.

Mom doesn't bother to answer, but Mrs. B. says, "Wait and see, Fritz."

"She means wait and freeze," Kathy says.

Mom opens the picnic basket and in the flash-light beam I see her set out some sandwiches, four cups, and a thermos. She passes us each a cup and says, "That jug Kathy brought is full of cocoa for you kids. We've got coffee. Here, you'll need a flashlight."

I hold it, and Kathy pours the cocoa. It's too hot to drink, but we wrap our fingers around the cups to warm our hands and let the steam warm our faces.

"What time is it now?" I ask.

"Three fifty."

Ten more minutes till—what?

"Ten minutes till we know," Mrs. B. says, almost like she's answering my question.

Till we know *what?* I take a sip of cocoa and burn my mouth.

Kathy says, "I'd rather be home in bed, wouldn't you?"

"Heck, no. I want to see what's going to happen."

Nobody says anything for a long time, and then Mom asks, "Now what time is it?"

The flashlight clicks on and Mrs. B. says, "Three minutes past four. They're late."

Who's late? I wish something would happen. The cocoa's cold now, and my feet are freezing. For something to do, I eat my sandwich. Kathy says I can have hers, and I eat it, too.

We've been sitting here for what seems like forever, with flashlights clicking on and off all around us like fireflies as people check the time. I hear somebody behind us say, "Four-thirty-three."

"More than half an hour late. How long do you think we should stay, Mona?"

Mom says, "We'd kick ourselves if it happened after we left, Marge. Besides, I don't want to drive back down that awful road in the dark."

We're going to be here till after daylight, then. I wonder what time the sun comes up. . . .

"Five-fifteen."

I blink and say, "The sun comes up at five-fifteen?"

"No, Fritz," Mom says. "That's what time it is now."

The sky is a deep gray instead of black, and I realize I must have fallen asleep sitting up.

"Five-fifteen and all is well, we hope," Mrs. B. says.

After a minute or so Mom says, "If nothing happens, at least we can be pretty sure everybody's safe. I'll be so glad when all this is over."

All *what?* The waiting, or the project? And then it hits me: Coming out here tonight has something to

212

do with the project! "Hey, Kath! Are you awake?"

"Yes, unfortunately."

I lean over and whisper, "Whatever we're waiting for has something to do with the secret project." And then I sit back and wait for her reaction.

For a minute I think she doesn't believe me, but then she pulls me toward her and whispers, "We're facing south, Fritz. You know what that means, don't you?"

The Trinity site! I feel like leaping up and yelling *BINGO!* But instead I whisper, "Good thinking, Kath," and I try not to mind that she was the one who put it all together.

We stare into the grayness and wait . . . and wait . . . and wait.

Suddenly the whole sky lights up. Somebody gasps, or maybe we all do. I hold my breath and soak it all up—the white flash that fills the sky and seems to last forever, the trees and mountains that look like purple cutouts in contrast to the eerie light behind them. And then nothing.

Nobody says a word. I don't think anybody even moves. We just sit here while the sky gradually turns from gray to pale blue, while the trees and mountains that had looked flat and purple take on their true shapes and colors. And then, one by one, people begin to gather up their things.

"That was really scary," Kathy whispers as we follow our mothers back to the car in the early morning light. "I wish I knew what it was. And what it means."

"It means the secret project is a success—they tried out the 'Gadget' and it worked." A feeling of relief sweeps over me, and I add, "It means the war's going to be over soon."

"When?" Kathy asks, grabbing my arm. "Before Matthew has to invade Japan?"

I pull away from her and say, "You make it sound like he'd be going in single-handedly or something." Matthew the Great against the Japanese Empire.

"Tell me if the war's going to end without our boys invading Japan, Fritz," Kathy says in a tight voice.

"Yes," I tell her, pretty sure I'm right. Isn't that why our fathers kept on working on the 'Gadget' after the Germans surrendered?

Now that it's light, I can look around and make a mental note of who else came out to stare into the distance from Sawyer's Hill. Looks like mostly scientists' wives. "Everybody seems kind of dazed," I say.

"Or else sleepy," Kathy says. "I can hardly keep my eyes open."

"Heck, I'd have stayed up all night for a chance to see that." For a chance to find out what they've been doing over in the Tech Area all this time.

Kathy gives me an exasperated look and says, "I wasn't complaining, Fritz. I was simply stating a fact." We climb into the back seat while our mothers finish loading the trunk with the blankets and other stuff they brought. While we're waiting for them, Kathy asks, "So are you going to put what we saw in History as I Experienced It, or in Notes on the Secret Project?"

"Both," I tell her, "but I'll write something different in each of them. See, I'll just describe what we saw in the history one, but in the one on the secret project, I'll say what I think it all means." I can hardly wait to get that notebook out of my closet!

As soon as our mothers get in the car to drive home, Kathy leans forward and says, "Mom! Fritz says this means the war's going to be over soon, and Matthew won't have to invade Japan."

My mother says sharply, "Where did you hear that, Fritz?"

"I didn't hear it anywhere—I figured it out."

Kathy's mom says, "You have a smart boy there, Mona."

"Too smart for his own good, sometimes," Mom says as she starts the car.

I glance over at Kathy to make sure she noticed that nobody contradicted what I'd said, but she's staring straight ahead with her fingers crossed. Thinking about her brother.

Mrs. B. rolls up her window to keep out the dust. "I'm glad we were two-hundred miles away from that blast, aren't you, Mona?"

Bingo! I finally found out how far away the disappearing fathers go when they leave here—now that they probably won't be going down there anymore.

When Mom stops the car in front of Kathy's building, she says, "Do you kids understand that you can't say a word to anyone about what you saw?" We promise that we won't, and then Mrs. B. makes us promise not even to talk about it to each other. I get the feeling she's wishing they hadn't brought us along.

As soon as we're back home, I say, "How did you know to go out there this morning, Mom? Did Dad tell you?"

Ignoring my question, she asks, "Want some

breakfast?"

"I'll fix myself something later. There's something I have to do."

"At this hour of the morning?"

"I've got to add what we saw to my History as I Experienced It notebook."

Mom's expression changes from surprised to serious. "According to what I've been hearing over at Tech, we just witnessed the dawn of a new age, Fritz," she says. "That's why Marge and I decided to take you and Kathy with us."

"I'm glad you did, Mom. And don't worry—we won't say anything."

In my room, I get History as I Experienced It out of my knapsack and write: "July 16, 1945: A new age dawned today when not long before sunrise a brilliant flash lit up the New Mexico sky about 200 miles south of Los Alamos."

I describe what we saw, and then I sit and think about it. It's hard to believe how many of us were watching from Sawyer's Hill. In spite of all the code words and the secrecy around here, a lot of people at least knew that *something* was going to happen—and that it would happen to the south.

I find Notes on the Secret Project in the stack of stuff on my closet shelf and open it to the Rumors and Observations section. After I write the date, I think for a minute, and then I get to work: "Some new kind of powerful explosive device was set off about 200 miles south of Los Alamos just before dawn this morning. This is what I think:

   1) It was a test of the 'Gadget' the scientists
      have been working on ever since they set

up the Lab here.

2) The 'Gadget' is probably some kind of
REALLY BIG BOMB.

3) That's why Dad and the other scientists
have been disappearing to the Trinity site.
All this time they'e been getting ready to
test their 'Gadget.'

4) Since it worked, now they can use it to
end the war."

And Kathy's brother won't have to invade Japan,
I think as I put both the notebooks in my knapsack.
Her brother and about a million other brothers and
sons and husbands, not that Kathy cares about them.

I wander back to the kitchen to fix some breakfast, and there's Mom, sitting at the table, frowning
into her coffee cup. "What's the matter? No milk,
again?"

She gives a start, and when she looks up I see
these lines on her face. Worry lines, like she had when
they thought Vivian might have polio. "Mom. What's
wrong?" I try to sound like Dad does when he wants
an answer right now and no excuses.

"Nothing, hon."

"Mom. Tell me." This time I put on a frown that
feels like Dad's frown looks, and it works!

She takes a deep breath and says, "I was thinking about your father. Wondering—" Her voice fades
away, but I know what she was going to say: Wondering if he's all right.

My knees feel so wobbly I sort of collapse into a
chair. Dad's chair. Suddenly I know how Kathy feels
when she worries about Matthew, why she doesn't
care about anything except whether her brother's

safe. Why the German surrender in Italy was more important to her than the end of the war in Europe.

My eyes meet Mom's, and I'm pretty sure we're both thinking the same thing. If the explosion was so bright this far away, what must it have been like *there*? If it was so much *brighter* than the sun, how *hot* must it have been?

I feel like I'm strangling. I manage to take a breath, but when I exhale it comes out like a sob. I pretend to have a coughing attack, and Mom gets me a glass of water, which I drink even though my stomach is in such a huge knot, there's probably no place for the water to go once I've swallowed it.

"All right now, hon?"

I nod, pretending that everything's fine, and she pretends to believe me. We sit there a bit longer, and then she sighs and says, "I guess I'd better get over to the Tech Area. What time did you say Jacob is coming by for you?"

"Oh, my gosh! I've got to pack a lunch—he'll be here any minute."

"Eat some breakfast before you leave. I don't want you hiking in the canyon on an empty stomach."

I'm about to say that I'll be hiking on my feet, but I think better of it. "Okay, Mom. See you later." She leaves, and after I pack a couple of sandwiches for lunch, I make another one to eat now. I've just finished choking it down when Jacob knocks.

I holler for him to come in, and the minute I see his face, I know. "You look like you must have gotten up pretty early this morning," I say.

"Yes. I stood by my window and looked at the night sky," Jacob says, his eyes on mine.

218

"Does your window face south?" I whisper, and he nods. I grab my knapsack and say, "Let's go." Even though Dad said Security wouldn't be listening in when the scientists aren't home, I'm not taking any chances. Especially now that they've got a file on me.

Jacob's father must be down at the test site, too, since he said "I" instead of "we," so when we get to the foot of the steps, I ask, "What did your father tell you before he left?"

Jacob says quietly, "He told me to look after my mother."

I feel a chill. "He was worried, then," I say, hoping Jacob won't think I'm asking him too many questions. Hoping Mom wouldn't think I'm breaking my promise, which I'm not, since she only said not to talk about what we saw.

"I think they were all worried. I realize now that Father and his friends were talking about the test when I overheard one of them say he feared the earth's atmosphere would ignite." Jacob gives a wan smile. "Obviously it did not."

"And they went down there anyway!" I exclaim. "You don't think of scientists needing courage, but I guess they do."

"All of us need courage, Fritz." Jacob lapses into silence, and I try not to mind that he had known ahead of time that something important was about to happen, that his father had at least told him to watch the sky south of here before dawn today. Again I wonder how Mom knew to watch from Sawyer's Hill. Was it because she works for somebody important in the Tech Area, or did Dad—

Dad. I clench my jaw as fear for my father's safety

threatens to sweep over me again. Maybe the atmosphere didn't ignite, but— I steal a glance at Jacob and see that he's watching me.

"It does no good for us to worry, Fritz," he says firmly. "Come. We will spend our energy hiking, instead."

The trouble is, it doesn't take much energy to worry. The trail down the canyon seems a lot more rugged than when Brownie's doing the walking, but concentrating on my footing doesn't keep me from wondering if Dad's okay. What if— I take a couple of deep breaths and tell myself to think about something else. How does Kathy stand it, worrying about her brother month after month? It's no wonder she's such a grouch.

Jacob's gotten pretty far ahead, and now he's waiting for me to catch up. For about the thousandth time, I wish I could ask him about how his family got out of Denmark. Dad told me that the Jews escaped in boats, and Sweden took them in. Setting out at night in some little boat must have taken a lot of courage—something I'm pretty short on. Heck, I don't even have the guts to face up to Lonny and Red. Or even just Lonny.

It's evening by the time Jacob and I get back from our hike, and I'm really beat. We say good-bye, and I drag myself up the steps to our apartment. Mom's home, and the first thing I notice is that those worry lines are gone from her face.

"Everything's fine," she says, "and your dad will be back late tonight. If you're not too tired, how about letting me treat you to dinner at the Lodge?"

"That would be great, Mom," I say, realizing that I no longer feel tired at all. For a minute, I think Mom's going to hug me, and if she does, I'm going to let her—just this once. But instead she roughs up my hair. I duck out from under hand and say, "Cut it out, Mom," because I know that's what she expects me to do.

She laughs and says, "Go get your shower. I'm hungry." Something about her voice reminds me of how Kathy sounded when she thought Matthew was coming home.

Chapter Twenty-Eight

Kathy watches me turn to the Rumors and Observations section of the Secret Project notebook and write: "Scientists are <u>still</u> disappearing from the Hill, and so far no one has come back."

"At least not any of the ones we know of," I say, as I put down my pencil.

Kathy gives me a superior look and says, "And you thought we'd found out everything there was to know when we saw the test of the Gadget last week."

"Yeah. Guess I was wrong."

"You were wrong about the war being almost over, too."

Her voice has this accusing tone to it, like it's my fault the fighting hasn't ended yet. When I don't answer, she says, "Aren't you even going to stick up for yourself?"

I shrug and ask, "How can I, when everything you've said is true?"

Kathy stands up and says, "You're impossible. I'm going home."

I watch her get up and leave, letting the screen door slam behind her. *She's* the one that's impossible. And not the only one, either—Mom's so irritable I can hardly say a word without getting my head bit off, and I can hear the next-door neighbors arguing. But not Timmy's parents. That's the thing that tipped me off that Timmy's dad was gone—how quiet it was downstairs. No deep voice rumbling, no Mozart and Beethoven symphonies late at night.

Timmy's father's a metallurgist, whatever that is. I already looked it up in the dictionary, and about all I found out is that it's some kind of scientist who deals with metal. Which I could have figured out on my own. So far, besides Timmy's dad, I know of two others who have left the Hill—two guys from ordnance that Kathy told me about. Don't know their names, 'cause all Kath heard was her mom saying that Mr. B. was overworked because two men from his division were away. Yesterday I thought Dad was gone again when he didn't show up for breakfast, but Mom said he'd been at the Lab all night.

I'm still staring at my open notebook and wondering what's going on when I hear Jacob knock, and I don't have to check my watch to know it's exactly 10:30. I holler that I'm coming and then lead him back to my room where yesterday's unfinished chess game is still set up. I turn the radio on to the community station, and before we start to play, I ask, "Has your father been staying over at the Lab till all hours the way mine has lately?"

Jacob hesitates a moment before he says, "My father left here several days ago. He said I was to be 'the man of the house' for the next few weeks."

Bingo! "Did he seem worried like he did before the big test?"

"He seemed—how do you say it—*resolute*, like a man with a job to do."

Lowering my voice, I say, "I don't get it. If they've already tested this 'Gadget' of theirs, what else is left

223

for them to do?"

"Now they must use it," Jacob says quietly. "It is your turn."

I move a pawn, and Jacob captures my bishop, saying sternly, "You are not concentrating on the game."

"Sorry. I was thinking about what we saw the other morning."

Jacob nods and says, "I think about it, too. The heat of the blast melted the desert sand into green glass. One of the neighbors brought some of it home as a—how do you call it?"

"A souvenir," I tell him, wondering how we can possibly use the gadget to win a battle without killing our own men.

"It is your move," Jacob says, and I quickly move a knight. In two more turns he says, "Checkmate."

He's right. I should have concentrated. I start to set up the board again, but Jacob stops me.

"We will play another day when your mind is on the game," he says, and he begins to put the chessmen in their box.

I don't want him to leave yet, so I say, "There's something I want to show you," and then I take the Secret Project notebook out of my knapsack and hand it to him. "Have a look at this," I say, and I turn the radio a little louder.

"'Notes on the Secret Project,'" he reads when he opens it. "This should be very interesting." I watch him read the list of names under Personnel and see his finger stop part way down the page. I figure he's come to his father's name, but he looks up and asks, "Did you know that the physicist you have listed here as Nicholas Baker is actually the famous Niels Bohr, who won the Nobel Prize in physics? We knew him well in Denmark."

I take back the notebook, and Jacob spells out the name for me as I write it in under the alias. "We know Enrico Fermi," I say, hoping to make up for not having heard of Niels Bohr. "He won the Nobel a couple of years ago, didn't he?"

Jacob nods. "In 1938. He, too, has an alias. My father says that when they travel, Enrico Fermi is known as Eugene Farmer."

"How come those two have aliases?"

"Because their immense knowledge is so important to the project," Jacob says, looking surprised that I'd asked. "The false names make it more difficult for enemy espionage agents to find and assassinate them."

Holy Cow! Searching car trunks at the gate suddenly starts to make sense. The inner fence around the Tech Area seems like a really good idea now, and so does having guards at the big shots' houses on Bathtub Row. As I hand the notebook back I say, "You know, it's pretty amateurish of Security to use aliases with the same initials as those scientists' real names. You'd think they could do better than that."

"Perhaps that is the only way they can remember who the men really are," Jacob says. He doesn't say anything else until he's finished the last page of the notebook. Finally, he closes it and asks, "How did you find out all of this?"

"Mostly by keeping my eyes and ears open. And then by using what I did know to figure out things I didn't know." I take the notebook from him, open it to Rumors and Observations, and on a blank page I write down what Jacob said about the heat of the test blast melting sand and about why the most famous scientists had aliases. Then I turn back to the page I started when Kathy was here and print: "Hermann Schwartz, a theoretical physicist, said he will be gone from the Hill for several weeks. The men who have left the Hill probably have something to do with using the Gadget to end the war."

Jacob reads this new part and says, "I would like to know where they have gone." I nod my agreement, and he adds, "When my father returns, I will find out and tell you so that you can make a note of it." He's looking at me with respect now, like he's forgotten my lack of attention to our chess game.

Too bad I never asked Jacob to work on the Secret Project notebook with me. Wonder why I worried that he'd think it was silly?

Chapter Twenty-Nine

Kathy's still complaining when she follows me off the bus. "I've never been so tired in my entire life," she says. "Don't bother to invite me next time you and Jacob go hiking, okay?"

I decide not to mention that she invited herself, and I don't ask why she didn't get off in front of her apartment instead of coming with me to the PX if she's so tired. Actually, I'm pretty worn out, too. It's a good thing those army buses will stop for you at a trailhead if you flag them down.

The newsstand at the end of the counter is empty, and I ask, "How come the papers are so late getting here?"

"You're the one that's late," the cashier says. "Papers went like hotcakes today. Knew they would, soon as I saw the front page, so I stashed one away for myself and put aside a couple others for some of my regulars." He reaches down behind the counter and pulls one out. "Here you go," he says, handing it to me like it was a present. "The very last paper on the Hill."

I stare at the headline that stretches all the way across the page until the cashier says, "You can take that with you, y'know. Soon's you pay for it." His words break the spell, and I count out the pennies and hand them to him.

Kathy's reading a Wonder Woman comic while she

waits for me, and I tap her on the shoulder and hold the paper so she can see the headline. "'U.S. Drops Atomic Bomb on Japan,'" she reads. "What kind of a bomb is that, exactly?"

"It's got to be what our fathers have been working on." I'm so excited the words sort of tumble out. "That huge flash we saw in the distance. From the hill where we skied. That had to be the test of this atomic bomb."

"Then the war will be over," Kathy says. "Matthew can come home."

But I barely hear what she's saying, because I'm staring at the words *Los Alamos,* written right here in the newspaper for everyone to see. "Look!" I whisper, pointing at it.

The two of us go outside and sit on the running board of a parked car while we read the entire article. When she finishes it, Kathy says, "And to think that our fathers did that." I can't tell whether she's awed or dismayed.

"The next big headline is going to tell us that the war is over," I say as we start toward home. When we get to our building, Timmy's mom waves and asks, "Did you kids hear the news?"

I hold up the paper. "We just read all about it."

Kathy and I say goodbye, and I hurry upstairs to show my parents the front page. They're sitting in the kitchen, a pitcher of iced tea on the table between them and their glasses still full. I hold the paper out to Dad and announce, "This is the very last copy on the Hill."

"I already saw it," he says, not looking up.

Mom adds, "They delivered a whole batch of papers over at Tech."

Quick footsteps on the stairs, then a knock, and as I go to see who it is, a small boy opens the screen door and slips in a sheet of paper. I pick it up and see it's some kind of notice. An invitation. I take it back to the table and say, "Everybody's invited to a party to celebrate."

Dad says, "I don't feel much like celebrating." His voice is toneless, like it was last winter when he was "low." I glance down at the newspaper, and when I think about what Kathy and I just read, I don't have to wonder why Dad's feeling "low" again.

"Dad?" I wait until finally he looks up. "Do you think dropping that bomb will help end the war without an invasion?" After what seems like a long time, he nods, and I say, "That means no more American boys will be killed, right?" When he nods again, I say, "Well, I don't know about you, but saving maybe hundreds of thousands of lives makes me feel like celebrating."

The kitchen is so still the hum of the refrigerator sounds loud. Finally, Dad says, "But what about the future?"

"The future?" Does he mean when the war's over?

"I don't like to think about the world your generation will inherit because of the work we did at the Lab," Dad says.

I have no idea what he's talking about, but Mom seems to. She leans forward and rests a hand on Dad's arm. "I think a lot of people on the Hill are worried about that, Verne. Today I overheard some of the scientists talking about staying here after the war ends. They want to use their influence to make sure atomic energy will be used in peaceful ways."

Peaceful ways? I'm so busy wondering what Mom means by that, I miss part of what she says next.

" . . . and maybe some kind of agreement for all the countries to sign—a promise never to make any kind of atomic weapons."

Without looking up, Dad says, "I know all about that, Mona. They asked me to join them."

Mom takes a deep breath and says, "If you want to stay on, I won't stand in your way, Verne."

"No, Mona, the genie is out of the bottle and beyond the reach of the scientific community now," Dad says. "It's in the hands of the military—the project has been their baby from the beginning, after all. Besides, I've had my fill of this place."

"How can you say that, Dad? This is a *great* place. I've learned a *lot* here." And I've made more friends than I've had in my entire life, up to now.

Dad meets my eyes for the first time. "It's been a great place for *you,* Fritz. And you'll always have what you learned here. Not only what you've recorded in your notebooks, but what you've learned about different kinds of people. And about yourself."

"But—"

"There are no but's about it, Fritz," Dad says. "We will not be staying in Los Alamos. And now I'm going to lie down."

When the bedroom door closes behind him, I plead, "Can't you make him change his mind, Mom?"

"You heard what he said. Your father came here to help do a job that had to be done, and now that job's finished. As soon as the war ends, we'll start making arrangements to go home—and it won't be a minute too soon. Do you realize that we've been away

230

from Vivian and your grandma for almost a year?"

I sit staring at the untouched glasses of iced tea, noticing the inch or so of paler liquid near the top where the ice has melted, until Mom reaches over and touches my arm. "I know it's going to be hard for you to leave the friends you've made here, hon, and I'm sorry," she says quietly.

Not half as sorry as I am. Without looking at her, I say, "I'll be in my room."

She probably thinks I'm in here sulking, I realize as I reach for my History As I Experienced It note-book, but first things first. I've got to write down some of that stuff Dad said before I forget any of it, and then I'm going to end the Secret Project notebook, 'cause the project isn't a secret anymore.

After I've done all that, maybe I'll sulk.

"I don't think Manny liked it much when you said he should ask Jacob to give him ping-pong lessons," I tell Kathy as we head toward the door of the PX after our doubles game.

"Too bad. He needs to improve. Ever notice that whichever side he's on always loses?"

At least it's not the side I'm on that loses. Unless, of course, Manny and I are partners, and then we'd be slaughtered if Jacob didn't insist on giving us a handicap. Maybe *he* can teach Kathy something about sportsmanship.

"Besides," she says, "if Jacob could turn you into a winner, think what he could do for Manny."

I ignore that and head for the newsstand. Kathy waits for me to buy a paper, and as we leave the PX, I say, "Looks like I was wrong again, Kath." Might as well own up before she has a chance to rub it in.

"Wrong about what?"

I point to the newspaper and say, "Three days ago, I told you the next big headline would say the war's over, but instead it's about dropping another one of those bombs on Japan."

I spread out the paper on the hood of a parked jeep so we can read the front page, but my eyes are fixed on one of the smaller headlines. "Look at this—they're calling Hiroshima 'a city of ruins and dead too numerous to be counted.' And now Russia's declared war on Japan. The Japanese are being attacked from all directions, and they still won't give up. Atomic bombs were supposed to end the war without an invasion, but—"

"Shut up, Fritz! Just *shut up.*"

She storms off, and I stand here trying to figure out what I said that upset her. Oh. The invasion. She doesn't want to think about it because of Matthew. I'm feeling like a heel, watching her walk along with her head down—crying, most likely—when I see Lonny and Red heading this way. Great.

Automatically, I crouch down beside the jeep. I don't think the two of them saw me, 'cause they were looking at Kathy. I tell myself they aren't going to bother a girl, but to make sure, I raise my head enough to see what's going on.

Uh-oh. They're bothering her. Standing in front of her and not letting her go by. She tries to go around them first on one side and then on the other, and they move over so she can't. And now they're saying something, taunting her for crying, I'll bet. How dare they! *And how can I let them?*

I come out from behind the jeep and head toward them. Not running, just walking fast. "Hey!" I shout. "You leave her alone."

All three of them are staring at me now, like they can't believe their eyes—or ears. I walk right up to them. Look straight at Lonny. Look straight at Red. Look back at Lonny and try to impale him on my gaze, the way Dad does with me when he means business, when he won't put up with any more nonsense.

"Let her go by," I say. "Now."

Nobody moves. It's like one of those Christmas pageants where people in angel and shepherd costumes stand around the manger while somebody reads the Bible story aloud. It's all I can do not to laugh.

Then Lonny takes a step forward, and I don't feel like laughing any more. "You gonna make me, Fritz?" he says.

I hold my ground. Right now I feel brave as a lion—and besides, Lonny sounded like he only challenged me because he thought Red expected him to. "Yeah," I say, and now *I* take a step forward. "I'm gonna make you, Lonny." I glare at him, and the flicker of uncertainty that crosses his face tells me that for once I've got the advantage. Keeping my eyes locked on his, I stick out my chin and clench my hands into fists. I concentrate on acting like a combination of Dad the time he caught me sneaking out to his car right after he drove the disappearing fathers' car pool and that mean MP when he was bullying Jacob at the PX. *And it works!*

Lonny shifts his eyes away from mine, and a feeling that's half power and half relief sweeps through me. I turn to Kathy and say, "Go on home, Kath."

She looks sort of dazed, but she manages to say, "Okay, Fritz." Red actually takes a step back so she doesn't have to walk around him.

I can hardly believe that I've won! When I turn to impale Lonny on my gaze again, he's watching Kathy walk away. He finally looks back to me, and I'm ready for him. "Don't bother her again, Lonny. Ever."

His eyes slide away from mine, and he seems to be studying the pavement, which makes me feel safe enough to turn my back on him—and Red—so I can get that newspaper I left on the ground over by the jeep.

I'm almost there when a GI picks up the paper and starts to read it. What the heck, I'll buy another one. I'm waiting in line to pay for it when Lonny and Red come in, heading for the pinball machines, no doubt. As they walk past, they glance at me, and I glare back at them and stick my chin out again—and that's it. Lonny doesn't sneer. Red doesn't make one of his snide comments. My heart beats a little faster, but my stomach doesn't tighten up at all. That feeling of power is gone, but I have still this incredible sense of relief, like a warm glow that's settled over me.

"Next!"

I put my pennies on the counter, and the cashier says, "Say, didn't you buy a paper a couple of minutes ago?"

"Yeah, but I let somebody have it, and I need another one."

I'm outside again before I realize the truth of what I told that guy—I really did let somebody have it. But not like Jacob when he was the Human Tornado. More like what Dad would have done.

Chapter Thirty

Jacob and I have finished our hike, and we're sitting by the edge of the road, waiting to flag down one of the army buses coming back to the Hill from Santa Fe.

"How much longer do you think the war's going to last?" I ask him. "I don't see how the Japanese can keep going after what we've done to them."

"You sound like you think atomic bombs should not have been dropped on their cities," Jacob says, frowning. "Do you think it is worse to burn to death many people at once with a single bomb rather than one at a time with blow torches as your Marines did on Iwo Jima?"

I finish the water in my canteen while I collect my thoughts. "Actually, I don't like to think of anybody being burned to death," I say, wishing Jacob didn't turn so many of our conversations into debates. "But those were *soldiers* on Iwo Jima, don't forget—soldiers who had been firing at our men from inside those caves on the island for weeks and weeks. My dad feels really bad that atomic bombs were used on civilians." Too late, I remember the firebombing of Dresden.

"When a country's leaders go to war, its people suffer," Jacob says in a flat voice.

Quickly changing the subject, I say, "When the war finally does end, we're going back to Indiana. I sure will miss this place when we have to leave."

"My father has decided that we will stay here," Jacob says, and I feel a surge of envy until I realize that his family has no home—and no relatives—to go back to. After a moment, he turns to me and says, "When we first came here, I hated the fences with their barbed wire and the passes we had to show. But I have learned that in spite of the military police and the soldiers everywhere, this is a safe place, and now I am glad that we will live here."

"I sure wish we were staying," I tell him.

"You want to fill up all of the notebooks you showed me?"

It sounds almost like Jacob's teasing, but in case he's not, I give him a serious answer. "Actually, filling my notebooks will take my whole life, because I start another one whenever I come across something interesting. Plus, I'll never finish my notebook on History as I Experienced It. I guess I'm through with Notes on the Secret Project though, since the project isn't secret anymore."

Jacob says quietly, "Perhaps you should start a second volume and call it The Aftermath of the Secret Project."

"Isn't that sort of a self-limiting subject? An aftermath is usually short, right?"

After the briefest hesitation, Jacob says, "Usually it is."

"So how long do you think this particular aftermath is going to last, anyway? I've already got a page called Postscript to the Secret Project."

This time, Jacob hesitates a little longer, but finally he says, "It might be years. Decades. It might even be forever."

Forever? "Are you thinking about what might happen if other countries learn how to make atomic bombs?" I ask him. "That's one of the things I've written about in my postscript—it's what everybody was talking about right after Hiroshima."

Jacob nods. "My father fears what he calls an 'arms race' among the nations, and he is concerned also about the dangers of radioactivity." He turns to me and asks, "Did you know that burns from radioactivity released in an accident in one of the laboratories will cost a scientist his life?"

"I heard a rumor about an accident in the Lab— it's in my postscript—but I just assumed the man was burned in a fire." And I didn't know he was going to die.

I'm about to change the subject when we hear the faint wail of a siren in the distance. A second siren joins in, closer, with a different pitch, and I hear Jacob catch his breath. I'm waiting for him to put his hands over his ears or something, but instead he says quietly, "I wonder how long it will be before I am no longer reminded of air raids each time I hear a siren."

Lately, sirens make me think of the day Manny and I ended up in that restricted area, and as more and more of them begin to howl, my mouth goes dry. *If I'm this nervous, how must Jacob feel?*

Suddenly I become conscious of a new sound—a furious honking. I look down the road and see a cloud of dust with a military police car inside it. The car goes on past, horn still blaring, then screeches to a stop. The driver slams it into reverse and stops again, opposite Jacob and me.

The MP in the passenger seat rolls down his window and yells through the dust, "It's over! The war's over! Hop in, kids."

Jacob looks as relieved as I feel, and we climb into the back seat. I'm thinking about how different this is from last time I rode in a police car when the MPs start to sing "The Star Spangled Banner." I join in, but Jacob just looks dazed. Suddenly a series of explosions stops our singing in mid-verse. Now the MPs are all business.

"Sounds like that came from one of the canyons," the driver says.

Above the pop-pop-popping of smaller explosions, the other MP says, "Probably some of those crackpot scientists, celebrating."

Celebrating because thanks to the bomb they helped build, our boys won't have to invade the Japanese home islands. Celebrating because Japan finally gave up.

The MPs let us out in the middle of town, and it's easy to tell that everybody's heard the news—lots of people standing around in groups, talking excitedly. Lots of cheering.

Kathy and Gail are headed toward the PX, and they wave. "Did you hear?" Kathy hollers as we go to meet them. "The war's over—Matthew's safe!"

Jacob says, "Now that the war is over, Kathy's brother is no longer in danger, Gail can go to the seashore, and Fritz will have another entry for his History as I Experienced It notebook."

My first thought is that he's poking fun, or at least making the point that the war hasn't really touched us. But Jacob isn't like that. Or is he? He's smiling, but it's the kind of smile I'd give somebody Timmy's age.

I guess the girls don't notice that, because Gail says, "Just think—our fathers helped win the war."

"They helped *end* the war," Jacob tells her. "The war would have been won without the bomb, but not yet. Not this soon."

"What do you mean, 'not this soon'?" Kathy says. "It seems like the war has been going on forever!"

Jacob nods in agreement. "Yes, and even longer for Europeans than for you here in America."

"Why are we talking about the war?" Gail asks. "We should be celebrating because it's finally over."

"Come on," Kathy says. "We'll celebrate with banana splits." And as we walk into the PX together, she announces, "I'm going to treat Fritz, because we never celebrated his own personal V-L Day." Jacob looks puzzled, so she adds, "Victory over Lonny," and then she tells him what happened, making me sound like some kind of a hero. Which is a big improvement over nobody mentioning that I'm a coward.

When she finishes her story, Jacob shakes my hand and says, "Congratulations, Fritz. I always knew that someday you would—how do you say it?—come to the end of your noose."

"Rope," we all say, correcting him.

Actually, I feel like I've finally got my head out of a noose.

Chapter Thirty-One

Last week, there were four of us around this same table here in the PX, having farewell sundaes the day before Gail left for California. And now, the day before I leave for Indiana, three of us are sitting here together, finishing up our farewell banana splits.

We don't seem to have much to talk about until Jacob turns to me and says, "I have meant to tell you where my father was those weeks he was gone. He was on an island in the Pacific, working with the team that assembled the bombs."

I get my Secret Project notebook out of my knapsack and turn to a fresh page. "It must have been Tinian Island," I say as I write FACTS on the top line, "'cause that's where the B-29s that dropped the bombs took off from."

"How did you know that?" Kathy asks.

"From reading one of Dad's news magazines." I should have been able to figure out where that batch of disappearing fathers had gone after the test blast as soon as I saw that article. I must be slipping. For a moment, I stare at the blank notebook page, and then I write: "The men who disappeared from the Hill after the test blast were part of the team that assembled Fat Man and Little Boy on Tinian Island in the Marianas, 1500 miles from Japan."

As soon as I finish, Kathy says, "Let me have your

notebook for a minute, okay?"

I hand it to her, and she writes something on the back of the last page. "My address," she says, clipping the pencil onto the cover and handing me the notebook. "We'll be pen pals."

I'm so glad she thought to give me her address that I don't even care that she's taking it for granted that I'll be her pen pal. "When Matthew comes home, you'll have to write me all about it," I tell her, surprised to realize that I really do want to know. And then I turn to Jacob and say, "P.O. Box 1663, Santa Fe, right?"

He nods, then turns to Kathy and says, "You must educate me about this 'being pen pals.'"

"It's just writing letters back and forth," she tells him. "You can have a pen pal you've never even met, just for something to do, or friends can be pen pals so they don't miss each other as much. So it's not a real goodbye when one of them leaves."

Her voice was sort of shaky on that part about missing each other, and Jacob looks like he wished he hadn't asked her. I feel a lump forming in my throat, so I cram the notebook into my knapsack. "Listen, I have to go now—but this isn't a real goodbye, okay?"

Kathy keeps on staring at the table, but she manages a faint "okay," and Jacob stands up to shake my hand.

After I leave the PX, I take a couple of deep breaths before I start walking toward Manny's place to tell him goodbye—a "real goodbye" this time, since Manny hates to write. And if I happen to meet up with Lonny on the way, I'll tell him goodbye, too. Goodbye, and good riddance. Or maybe goodbye and good luck, 'cause a kid like him is going to need all the luck he can get.

"You think they'd let me keep my pass instead of turning it in when we leave?" I ask as we approach the gate.

"I seriously doubt it, son. What would you do with it?"

"I could paste it on the cover of my Secret Project notebook."

Dad pulls over to the side of the road and stops the car. He tips the rearview mirror so he can look me in the eye and says, "Let me see if I understand. You're planning to ask the MP at the gate if you can keep your pass and paste it on the cover of your Secret Project notebook?"

"Actually, I thought maybe you could ask if they'd let—"

"Fritz. Where is that notebook now?"

I hold up my knapsack and say, "In here."

"Keep it in there. Do you understand?"

I nod, and Dad readjusts his mirror and pulls back onto the road. "The last thing I need is another delay at the gate because of that son of yours, Mona. I want to put this place behind me."

"So do I," Mom agrees. "It's been a difficult year."

In my mind, I contradict her. *It's been a great year.* In spite of Lonny and Red, this has been the best year of my life.

We stop at the gate, and Dad rolls down the window. When he hands over our passes he says, "You can keep those. We're checking out."

242

The MP spreads them into a fan and glances at each of us like he's making sure we're not imposters. When his gaze stops on me, I feel a jolt of recognition—he's one of the MPs who questioned me about the "Please Expedite" envelope. The young, friendly one. He motions for me to roll down the window. Great. Now what?

He holds out my pass and says, "You want this for a souvenir, Fritz?"

"Yeah, sure! Thanks." I take it from him, scarcely believing my luck, and then he shakes Dad's hand and wishes us a safe trip home—just like a regular person.

After we drive through the gate for the last time, Dad says, "Tell me more about this Secret Project notebook of yours, Fritz."

I'm about to start in, but Mom says, "I do not want to hear a single word about anything to do with the secret project. I am sick of the project."

"I'll let you see the notebook when we stop for the night, Dad. Maybe you can tell me some of the things I couldn't figure out, like what those ambulances with the police escorts were bringing to the Lab."

I see Dad's fingers tighten on the steering wheel. "Plutonium," he says. "For 'Fat Man,' the Nagasaki bomb. But how—"

Mom puts her hands over her ears and says, "If the two of you don't change the subject immediately, I am going to scream."

"We'll talk tonight, son," Dad says, and I tell him okay, but I'm thinking *Bingo!*

Mom takes her hands off her ears and says, "Thanks, you two—that's much better." Then she looks back at me and says, "Now that we're going home, you can be Franklin again, hon."

Franklin? Wasn't he that kid back in Indiana—the one who didn't have any friends? The one who was always being picked on? I hold up my pass and point to last year's photo and say, *"This* is Franklin, Mom. I'm Fritz."

Historical Note

When scientists in the United States began working on the atomic bomb, their goal was to develop a superweapon before the Germans beat them to it. It was up to them to make sure it was the Allies and not the Nazis who harnessed the power of fission.

The Germans surrendered in May 1945, but the U.S. was still at war in the Pacific. Even though Japanese leaders had lost all hope of winning, they swore they would never surrender. It looked like the war might go on for another year.

Meanwhile, American sailors were dying when Japanese pilots dive-bombed their ships with "kamikaze planes." American soldiers and marines were dying in fierce battles for the Pacific Islands. American pilots were being lost in bombing raids. So the scientists at Los Alamos continued their work on the superweapon. Now their goal was to end the war in the Pacific. Bombing Japan would end the war quickly—and without an invasion that could mean hundreds of thousands more dead and wounded.

When an atomic bomb was tested in the New Mexico desert, heat from the explosion melted sand and vaporized a steel tower. This made some of the scientists question using such a weapon against a city. When they were trying to learn the secrets of the atom and to find a way to harness its power, these men had been involved in pure science—in intellectual problem-solving. Now, they saw the terrible destruction that could result from their work.

But there could be no turning back. Once the United States had atomic weapons, how could its leaders justify *not* using them to end the war?

"Little Boy," the first atomic bomb, was dropped on Hiroshima on August 6, 1945; "Fat Man," the second atomic bomb, was dropped on Nagasaki on August 9; and on August 14, Japan surrendered.

Like Americans everywhere, the scientists at Los Alamos celebrated when the news of the surrender came. They were relieved that the war was finally over, and they were proud that their work had helped bring it to an end. But the scientists were also convinced that atomic weapons must never be used again. They wanted nuclear energy to be under international control. And they wanted it to be controlled by scientists—not by military or political leaders.

But the men who worked for international control of nuclear energy found that their loyalty to the United States was questioned. And they soon saw their fears realized as an arms race began. One by one, other countries become nuclear powers. And then all of the nuclear powers began to build atomic bombs as fast as they could—and to develop weapons that were even more powerful. Back in August of 1945, few Americans asked whether bombing Japan was the right thing to do—or if it was really necessary. But as the years went by, both ordinary people and their leaders looked back and began to ask these questions—and to form opinions and to argue with each other.

Today, historians are able to read government and military records that both Japan and the United States kept secret for fifty years. Now when people argue about dropping the A-bomb, they will have more facts to back up their opinions. Or maybe the facts will make them change their opinions.

But what of the scientists who worked on the bomb? Did living in "the aftermath of the secret project" change the way they felt about their part in developing the first atomic weapons?

At a reunion on the fortieth anniversary of the opening of the Lab at Los Alamos, one of the scientists (I. I. Rabi) said that the creators of the bomb shouldn't feel guilty because atomic energy has been misused. "What we did was great, what we did was inevitable; what we did was fortunate for the United States, and for the world—as of that period."

Another scientist (Victor Weissokopf) seemed to agree when he said, "Forty years ago we meant so well, but it did not turn out so well."

How would it have turned out if the scientists hadn't succeeded in creating the bomb? How would it have turned out if the bomb hadn't been used?

We will never know the answers to these questions. But we *do* know that the success of the secret project has affected the United States and the world in ways no one could have predicted—or imagined.